SEVEN TOWNS

and

SEVEN RIVERS

The Maiden Crossings

Anen' Martin

ISBN 978-1-0980-2795-7 (paperback)
ISBN 978-1-0980-2796-4 (digital)

Copyright © 2020 by Anen' Martin

All rights reserved. No part of this publication may be reproduced, distributed, or transmitted in any form or by any means, including photocopying, recording, or other electronic or mechanical methods without the prior written permission of the publisher. For permission requests, solicit the publisher via the address below.

Christian Faith Publishing, Inc.
832 Park Avenue
Meadville, PA 16335
www.christianfaithpublishing.com

Printed in the United States of America

It was an August afternoon when Simeon walked into the Eclectic Sculptors, a tattoo salon, to get a certain design tattooed on his leg. It was a picture that had, for long, existed only in his mind; he could not have imagined he was about to take a step that would forever alter his life. After all, since when was it routinely life-threatening that getting a tattoo from a licensed tattoo facility was something one had to be overly concerned about. Surely, it is widely understood that the art of living, in itself, has inherent risks; but not even Simeon could have predicted that his life, or anyone's life for that matter, could have predicted that his life, or anyone's life for that matter, could have been so profoundly altered by a single normal event. For a long time, Simeon had concluded that if he ever had to get a tattoo, it would be the one image that he has had in his mind for a long time.

  The image first appeared in his dream one cold afternoon when he dozed off after a cup of warm tea. The mental image of it had it looking like one of the ancient Greek gods but with two horns and eyes that conveyed omniscience. In his dream, the figure he would later call "Zeus" stood in front of a couch with its eyes fixated at him while he slept. He had dozed off right at the table where he had the tea with his head resting on the table. As strangely as it seemed, he was not disturbed, nor did he read anything unruly into it. The only aspect of it that seemed somewhat out of place was that even when he repositioned his head during the sleep, the same image appeared again with him lying in a couch while Zeus stared down his dormant body.

  In the event that he would later have a change of mind and decide to remove the tattoo, he decided he would never have more than one. He had never fancied wearing tattoos all over his body as he never really thought it carried with it much decency nor conveyed much respect. Nevertheless, he was drawn to the image he called Zeus and decided to immortalize it by having it carved on his leg.

The first pinch as the tattoo tool penetrated his leg was more painful than he anticipated, but the pain quickly dissipated. It was somewhat surprising that there was no feeling at all as he maintained his position to the end while the tattoo needle buzzed through his leg. Despite the ease with which the process advanced, he felt very weak and nauseated when he got to his feet. He felt drained, his heartbeat irregular, and the left side of his head throbbed. The more Simeon looked at the object that was just tattooed on his leg, the one that had existed only in his mind until now, the more it seemed to look back at him. It did not matter from which angle he looked. He was content with the artwork and thought it was flawless and had no variation from the way it had existed in his imagination.

Adhering to the way he felt, he decided to go home, putting aside everything else he had planned for the day. When he made it to his house, he felt very thirsty, and his urge to consume some water was overwhelming. He did exactly that, and by the time he stopped, he had consumed well over two quarts of water and fell asleep shortly afterward.

As he looked at the clock upon waking up, he realized he had slept for eight hours in the same position he had laid down. He once again consumed another large quantity of water, then sat down to wonder about the dream he had, why he slept for such a long time, considering he slept well the night before. Over all, he felt refreshed, vigorously energized. It was as if some new strength had descended upon him, and his every step was sure-footed.

As he leaned back on the couch with his head resting on the top, as if he were looking at the ceiling, he relived the dream he had while he was asleep. It was a long dream, and the more he thought about it, the more it occurred to him that the dream was more like a trip that lasted the length of his sleep. The more he recalled the dream, the more it baffled him as he tried to make some meaning of it all.

He was walking through the middle of a dirt road as people that seemed strange and remarkably different passed by him on both sides going the opposite direction. The soil was not the kind he had ever seen in real life nor seen in books or movies. It was somewhat dusty, light-yellow colored, with brushes on both sides. None of the plants resembled anything he had ever known or seen before. He recalled that he was the only one going the direction he was, and everyone else the opposite, and that he was unable to make any eye contact with any of them. There were old men with gray beards. Some of them were walking with canes; others had their canes resting on their shoulders with both hands resting on them. It seemed he walked a very long distance for a very long time with the scene repeating itself. The trees were the same and so were the tall brown shrubs, dry with no leaves.

These creatures (he was not sure if they were normal humans) seemed the same even though he was never able to focus on any of them. There were some light-yellow clouds of dust that impeded clarity between his position and theirs, but they walked upright on two feet. He did not attempt to talk to any of them, and none of them showed any acknowledgement of his presence. It was as if he was not there. He wondered if any of them saw or noticed him, and if so, what they might have thought of him. Some of them appeared to have been women with little children walking by their sides, all looking toward the same direction.

It was very clear to Simeon that he stood out. It was not enough that it was a completely strange place, but by every account, he did not belong there. The more he thought about his dream, the more he wondered if there was any meaning to any aspect of it. He remembered he had a vague idea of a destination he thought he would soon get to, but no sense of what or where it was. As he sat there retracing the dream, he felt thirsty. He got up to fetch himself another unusually large dose of water and emptied it down his stomach. He sat back on the couch again only to fall asleep before he even realized he was sleepy.

Upon waking up, Simeon felt very agitated that he slept yet another three and a half hours not long after an eight-hour sleep. Even more so that he had what he termed "the same dream," a dream that once again put him on the same dirt road he trekked in his prior dream. He stood there in the room, gazing on the floor as if to find an answer to the puzzles in his brain. Then he stared straight through the window with both hands crossed over his head. He wondered about the sleep, then the dream, his thirst for water, why he was not frequenting the bathroom to urinate considering the amount of water he had consumed, then the sleep again—on and on.

Although he thought it was odd to have pretty much the same dream twice, it seemed even more so to him that this second time around, he walked by someone he was sure to be blind; however, the seemingly blind very much maintained a long stare at him as he approached. He was sure the man had no eyes. There was no sign he had any eyeballs, only deep emptiness in the sockets where the eyeballs were supposed to be. Yet he seemed to have been looking at him up to the time he stopped in front of him, staring at his face without eyes. Is that even possible? What was he looking with? He quizzed himself without any obvious answer. Behind the eyeless blind man, there was something like a miniature cyclone, a collection of what seemed to Simeon like dust spinning around just on one spot while a headless falcon walked continuously counterclockwise around the cyclone.

The more he tried to sort through the dream, the less sense it made to him. The strangeness of it led him to become wary of even sitting or lying down on any surface out of fear that he might fall asleep again and have the same dream. He blinked several times as if to reassure himself that his eyes were not heavy, that he was not about to fall asleep. He decided to get out of his apartment, perhaps because he feared sitting down and getting thirsty would result in drinking yet more water, or falling asleep and waking up after another unpleasant dream.

He proceeded to his closet to change. As he bent down to remove his shorts, he noticed a continuous throbbing right in the middle of his tattoo. It was like watching a healthy human heart visibly at work. For a good while, as he kept his gaze on it, he could not help being astonished as it throbbed on with absolutely no sensation whatsoever. He was not feeling anything and would not have known of it had he not looked. He wondered how long that had been going on. He felt mystified as to how he did not physically feel anything. He put his hand over the tattoo, feeling the throbbing but not much else. He shut his front door behind him and walked out into the night.

As he left his apartment, Simeon was not sure where he was going. He did not particularly have a destination in mind; he only wanted to go for a stroll. He just wanted to get out of his apartment, thinking he needed some fresh air. Indeed, he was scared to sit in the apartment and possibly relive the prior episodes of dreams he had become wary of.

He was surprised to see that the streets were livelier and bustling with nightlife activities than ever before. As he turned a corner and into the street below the overpass of a major highway, there were different groups of individuals enjoying the nightlife under the bridge. He walked past a group of five young men that were having some disagreement, immersing themselves in a physical exchange while one of them, it seemed to him, was not having any success inducing a truce. He slowed down to look at them while making his way across to wherever his intuition was directing him. He was happy to find himself out there, and the busyness and liveliness of the outside engendered some enthusiasm.

"You better keep on going, buddy," yelled the big chubby guy that looked like a small-town bully. He seemed out of control as Simeon watched him continuously charge against some among his group while it seemed that the appeal from some to taper it down was unproductive. He was beyond adherence to any measure of restraint. He barely finished barking his orders before he picked up an unopened can of soda and launched it against Simeon with all the strength he could muster.

In what seemed like a lightning speed of reflex, Simeon caught the can and launched it right back at the source, hitting him very hard on the right front shoulder. It happened so fast that Simeon himself could not believe his own reflex and the level of agility with which he responded. *What the...?* he thought to himself, not even able to imagine what or how that could have been possible. It was nothing that he ever experienced before. The reflex and the precision with which he responded were beyond his own comprehension.

It seemed that the group that was just fighting each other was about to unite against him. He quickly realized that he had just served himself up as their common enemy. His presence has brought in the resolution they sought. They all launched toward Simeon, all five of them, speedily without hesitation.

Common sense would dictate that one against five was perfectly an odd match against the one person, that the lone defender ought to at least make a run for an escape. Instead, Simeon charged toward them defiantly, leaping some six feet high to sink both his feet into the face of the one that threw the soda can at him. Landing with his hands on the shoulders of the second person and swiftly turning him, he then pushed his head forcefully against the head of the third person.

Having seen the speed and agility with which things transpired, one of the remaining two so far untouched took himself out of contention as quickly as his legs could carry him. He ran out into a parking area across the street. Right on his heels was the other who equally felt he was better off taking himself out of the fight since he was so far untouched, glancing behind him as he ran. Both quickly got into a vehicle as what seemed to them as a faint police siren was becoming a little louder. As they steered the vehicle toward their friends, three of them quickly jumped into the back of the Isuzu truck and made their way out.

While Simeon was looking toward the direction of the siren, the small-town bully once again launched a piece of two-by-four he picked up from the truck bed against him as they fled, hitting him squarely on his tattoo. He watched as an ambulance raced down the road with its siren blaring.

*****

It has been four days since Simeon had his tattoo. He was also growing accustomed to unusually strange dreams. The dreams were now becoming more like out-of-body experiences, more and more like real-life phenomena. He found himself leaving his body shortly after another large dose of water. This time he traveled past the blind man with a barn that had a headless falcon and eternal mini cyclone.

The more he walked, the more it seemed there was a large body of water in the horizon. He felt his left leg itching—his tattoo. He raised his leg and rubbed it only to notice some dark-green fluid in his fingers. He was surprised to see some fluid coming from each of the eyes of the tattoo figure as he examined it. The fluid was red but immediately turned dark green upon wiping it off. From the tattoo, they dripped like teardrops coming from each eye. It was as if the tattoo figure was crying but shedding blood for tears, blood that rapidly turned into something else.

Suddenly, he felt the urge to go back, but instead of turning around, he walked backward so effortlessly that it seemed so natural. He had always walked straight during other out-of-body experiences, but this time, walking backward, he turned left and kept walking until he came to a stop. A house stood behind him.

Simeon woke up clutching his left hand. It was very painful as he clenched and unclenched the fist repeatedly. Despite the pain, he managed to exercise the hand like that repeatedly to ensure that circulation was not lacking. It was still painful as he sat on his bed, wondering about his dream.

He noticed that one of his fingernails was broken. By his estimation, some effort must have been required for the fingernail to break the way it did. The tips of his fingers were sore and reddish; they appear swollen. The back of his hand had a thin straight cut that he'd swear was not there when he went to sleep. The more he examined his hand, the more dumbfounded he became. He thought through his activities of the day and was unable to recall any task he might have undertaken to account for the condition of his hand and fingers.

He recalled that his dream, or his out-of-body experience, ended when he stopped after walking backward for some time. He recalled that he truly only felt that there was a house behind him when he stopped, not that he really saw one for sure. He also recalled that as he stood there, everything in front of him gradually faded away in slow-motion. It was more like everything from where he stood drifted backward in a gradual motion until all he could see was a cloud of light-yellow dust.

*****

The police investigating the death of Mr. Willard approached it from a cult-killing standpoint, although his ripped-out liver was lying next to the body. No missing body part or further mutilation was visible. Those who argued that it was not cult-related explained that some body parts would have been missing if it had anything to do with cultism. They added that it could not possibly be just to get some human blood; otherwise, they would have done so by simply severing one of the major blood vessels.

When they interviewed some friends of the deceased, they only gathered that the victim, along with some of his friends, engaged in a physical altercation a few nights ago with someone that fought like a monster. They were unable to provide any helpful description of the person. They provided information on where the fight took place and explained that they ran away when they thought the police were heading for them below the overpass.

The investigating detectives pulled the videos of all the intersections covering the location where the fight took place, two hours to the time and two hours afterward. They picked up Simeon after Mr. Willard's friends had identified him. It did not matter how many times or how loudly he proclaimed his innocence; he was detained and later charged for murder.

In his trial, the prosecutors showed videos of Simeon as he walked through two intersections, concluded that he took time to find where the deceased lived, then went and not only killed him but did it so monstrously. Although the prosecutors offered no evidence of forced entry into the victim's residence nor produce anyone that saw the accused, they stuck to their conclusion.

Simeon's attorney fiercely demanded that the prosecutors produce the murder weapon, explain how the defendant got into the house, and, most of all, produce videos of the intersections of the defendant's area of residence showing the times and activities in his own area. He also demanded the prosecutors produce the videos of the victim's area to show his client's presence as they alleged. He argued that the government is never interested in actual and true justice, but only concerned with winning its case at all costs even to the extent that nonconforming pieces of information are inherently suppressed or altogether, thrown out, "thereby murder justice from the get-go."

"No one here is arguing that a crime did not take place, a gruesome one at that. There is no conjecture whatsoever on whether a crime has taken place. My contention here, however, is that before anyone is convicted for any crime, we want to make sure that such a conviction was obtained in the fairest way possible. It is incumbent on all of us," he argued, "to ensure that such a conviction has its merit within the legal boundaries we profess. Let's not forget that this defendant," pointing to Simeon, "is someone's child, just as the victim was."

He argued fiercely without yielding to request for caution in his utterances. When the day's arguments were concluded, the defendant was remanded back into jail and request for bail was denied.

Just a few minutes after the court reconvened, the defendant, sitting in the third seat by the right side of his attorney, repeatedly asked for water, emptying one glass after another as quickly as he was handed one. The defense attorney advised the court that the charge against his client has taken a terrible toll on him and as such has not been feeling very well. He pleaded for the court to accommodate the defendant's condition during the proceeding and to accord him every right due a human despite his standing as the accused.

Simeon rested his forehead on the table in front of him as the proceeding went on. As he lay there half awake and half asleep, he heard the prosecuting attorney inform the court that he did not have any of the traffic videos the defendant's attorney had requested. He added that he had not been privy to any video other than the one he tendered to the court, which was also subsequently shared with the defense attorney. Just before he could ascertain if he was asleep or awake in the courtroom, Simeon found himself walking the dusty path once again.

Some forty-five minutes into the prosecutor's rendition, he was approached, and a piece of paper was handed to him by a member of his prosecuting team. "It's about your son. Please come to the school immediately" was the message on the piece of paper. He asked the judge permission to approach the bench. After a brief discussion, the prosecutor and the defense attorneys agreed for the court to adjourn for the time being. The defendant was once again remanded back into jail.

The night before, as Simeon was in deep sleep, he found himself walking through some alleys, making some rigorous turns until he reached behind a seven-story building after a brief turn to his left. He made his way into the building from a rear entrance, passed right in front of some armed security men, and continued to the third floor of the building. From a long, richly carpeted hallway, he turned and stood in front of what seemed like an elegant conference room. He found himself inside the room, although the door never opened. The five men in the room, including the chief prosecutor and three women, were interrupted in their discussion when some papers that were lying on the table were blown and scattered all around the room, even though none of the doors or any of the windows were open. They looked at each other and around the room to see that nothing else was out of place.

Mr. Mangioni, the chief counsel prosecuting the case, was reviewing the information that his team would use in the court proceeding, sorting out what to use and what to destroy. As they all dispersed themselves in the conference room to pick up the papers that were tossed around, the lights in the room flickered for about seven seconds, then the room went dark. When the lights came back on, one of those in the conference room called the security desk and asked what the problem was. "Which lights? What problem?" the person at the desk responded and added that they did not notice any abnormality with the lighting.

Mr. Mangioni continued with their discussion. He explained to the rest of his team that since they had no other suspect for the murder of Mr. Jeff Willard, they had to make this stick. "Anything and everything that points away from him must be removed from our presentation. The videos that do not support our position will be destroyed, so we won't have to present them to the defense."

He went on to say, "As prosecutors, justice is only served when our arguments prevail. It has nothing to do with actual facts because when our arguments prevail over that of the defense and the jury sides with us, then that not only becomes the fact, but it also establishes itself as the truth, and therein lies justice."

He called his son's school as soon as he left the courtroom, but Mr. Mangioni was advised to go home, that the police were on their way to meet him at his residence. There, as he sat with his wife, two police officers and one official from the school informed the parents that their son's body was found in the school bathroom with an internal organ ripped out of the body. "He's dead. I'm sorry. The authorities, along with the school administrators, have mounted an intensive investigation into the incident, and we're hopeful we will uncover every detail," the Mangionis were told. Two days after the news of his son's death, Mr. Mangioni suffered a severe stroke. He lost the control of his bodily functions and required around-the-clock assistance.

When the court reconvened, Simeon's attorney, aware of the prevailing situation, asked the court to acquit his client. He cited that, "There are occultists, or some devil worshippers out there bent on committing some horrific crimes, and my client has nothing to do with that at all. Unless someone can prove to us that he was not locked up in his cell when the recent murder occurred, an exact repeat of what he's accused of and being tried for. I therefore ask that the court dismiss this case with prejudice."

Simeon was happy to go home following his acquittal and release from detention. The more he thought about his unusual abilities, the more he grew accustomed to them, and he was also beginning to relish the newfound energy. During his interrogation about the murder of Mr. Jeff Willard, when he submitted to the authorities' demand that he take a polygraph test, he responded that he had nothing to do with the murder and concluded that he answered every question truthfully. Mr. Mangioni tossed out the polygraph when the result supported Simeon's claim; he only advised the court that the result was inconclusive when the defendant's attorney demanded the result be made available to him.

Simeon was very happy to be in the company of his friends, enjoying the party they organized in his honor to celebrate his freedom. They were all enjoying the gathering and each other's company, eating, drinking, and just having a good time. The more the party intensified, the noisier it became.

As it got louder, Michael was ridiculed when he swore that he noticed Simeon's tattoo blink at him. He said he saw the tattoo look up at him and then blinked.

"No more alcohol for you tonight, dude," another friend responded.

"No. I swear. I'm not drunk. I know what I saw. It moved its eyes, man," he repeated strongly in an attempt to convince them that he was neither drunk nor lying.

Everyone else that looked at the tattoo was unable to notice anything to support Michael's claim. Andy went to Simeon's refrigerator, then came back to Michael and said, "Here's the only thing you need to drink for the rest of the night. You're a pussy and not man enough to handle alcohol." He left a gallon of water by Michael's side. He felt ridiculed but did not make an issue out of the exchange.

As they loudly traded words back and forth, they heard some bangs on the door. Three men in police uniform forced the door open just as it was cracked open from the inside. The door smashed against Alvin's face and broke his nose. While he was clutching his broken nose, he was ordered, along with the rest of the people in the room, to keep his hands up; and they were all searched one by one and ordered to end the party or face immediate arrest with severe charges. "Whose place is this?" they demanded.

"I live here," Simeon responded.

"Is there any firearm in this place?" one of the police officers queried.

"I don't own any firearm."

"That's not what I asked. Let's try it again," the police ordered. "Is there any firearm in this place?"

"There's no firearm in this place."

The three police officers looked around, and then left.

They quickly attended to Alvin's nose and decided to just end the party and go home. Andy and Alvin were the first to grab their coats and leave since they both came in the same car, but they quickly came back to alert the others that police vehicles were outside, perhaps waiting for them to stop and arrest them for drunk driving. Simeon suggested they all spend the night since it was almost three o'clock in the morning. They were happy to make themselves comfortable and not render themselves the bait for what they termed "government forces."

They were all awakened by loud sirens that at first, sounded like that of the fire trucks. But as it intensified, almost all of them went to the windows to peep to see what was going on. It became clear that something big must have been going on as several police vehicles, emergency medical services, and fire trucks were speeding through the access road heading west of Simeon's apartment. It was seventeen minutes past nine Saturday morning.

They were all awake now, all sitting up while Simeon was in the kitchen, trying to put together something in the name of breakfast for everyone. By the time he was through, the foam that once chambered a dozen and a half eggs was now in his trash bin, along with some wraps that only a moment ago held together three loaves of sliced white bread. Everyone sat wherever was comfortable as milk and juice cocktail containers changed hands. It was not long before the event of the early morning police visit was introduced into their conversation. Kenny said his father once told him: "In the past, the police used to be public servants instead of our masters."

"And what exactly was all that about you having a gun here or not?" Andy asked Simeon.

"I wish I knew," Simeon responded.

"Maybe he wanted to know if you are one of the gun nuts," Aaron said. "You've got to know that if you're a gun-worshipping son of a bitch with all of us in here, having had more beer than Satan, we could have easily taken them on and really do some damages."

"As far as I'm concerned, I could never have too many guns. One needs to have the means to defend oneself," Michael added.

"One gun is all you need to defend yourself, my friend. After all, it's not like you're going to have an army invade you."

"Excuse me? Who said you could never be invaded by an army. Have you been sleeping lately?" Michael argued forcefully. "And if you're invaded what chance exactly would you have? The answer is none. At least I'd have a fighting chance."

Aaron laughed. "Right before you die?" he asked.

"Well, if they must kill me, I'm going to be hell-bent on taking as many of them with me as possible."

Aaron laughed again.

"It may sound funny to you. And yes, go ahead and laugh. People like you are content taking whatever orders that the government dictates. I just happen to not be that naive, my friend."

"But, Michael, you are awfully the naive one, I'm sorry to say."

"No sir, you—"

"Hold on, let me break it down to you. Just listen for a minute—"

"For just a minute, listen," Aaron pleaded. "Let me ask you, where exactly are you planning on waging this war from? It certainly would not be from a far-off open field in the middle of nowhere. Therefore, that only means it's going to be from your house. So I ask you. What exactly do you have in your house that gives you this illusion that you can stand and engage in a gun battle with government forces if they want to take you down?

"My friend, we all live in houses that are nothing but a pack of highly flammable wooden two-by-fours begging to go down at a strike of a match. You make it sound like these government forces that will invade you are going to show up at your front door with bayonets drawn.

"Let me tell you," Aaron continued, "if you ever become that much of a threat to the government, or your house ever that much of a threat, trust me, you will be picked up or taken out in the middle of a freeway without your feet even touching the ground.

"Sir, I am not the naive one. I remain cognizant of the fact that this government possibly knows when everyone of us even takes our showers. It got out of hand a long time ago, and none of the gun-worshippers raised their guns to put a stop to it. All we heard and continue to hear are useless rhetoric while the band plays on. Get a life."

He got up, went to Simeon's kitchen, took a plastic drinking cup, and went to the gallon of water Andy had brought out during the party. He picked it up, but the gallon was empty.

Just as Aaron was about to ask what happened to the water, Simeon's front door came off the hinges, crashing some three feet into the living room. Somewhat reminiscent of a well-rehearsed invasion, all the windows in the apartment simultaneously breached from the outside, with glasses completely shattered, and the bathroom door broken in two pieces even though it was not locked. In what seemed less than a minute, the apartment was swamped with government forces that spared no time roughing up everyone in the apartment. The young men, all of them handcuffed, were marshaled outside to be transported separately to a detention facility where they would be housed in separate cells.

*****

They were interrogated separately in their individual cells, each of them to near exhaustion. Not all went well in Simeon's cell as his interrogator started off by calling him a criminal that escaped justice and made it clear that his luck has run out this time around.

"I don't understand," Simeon replied.

"Let's hope someone will still recognize you by the time we're done with you. Maybe your mother will identify you by your stupid tattoo when the dust has settled. You've had your run."

"Excuse me?" Simeon asked. "Don't you bring my mother into whatever racket it is that you're running. Worry about your own mother and let me worry about mine."

The interrogating detective became infuriated. He gazed at Simeon with utter disgust, and his red countenance filled with rage. If he could summarily execute Simeon and not be inconvenienced, he certainly would. He abruptly left the cell.

"You are being moved to another cell. Turn around and put your hands above your head," officer O'Connor ordered Simeon when he returned to the cell with a set of handcuffs.

Simeon turned around with his hands above his head. "Are we allowed to contact anyone?" he asked but did not get a response as both his hands were bound together by the handcuffs. Instead, he was swiftly turned around toward the entrance of the cell with Officer O'Connor's left hand gripping the back of his neck.

He kicked Simeon violently on his spine. "That way," he pointed toward the entrance of the cell as he very briefly let go of his left hand from Simeon's neck.

"What the hell is that all about?" Simeon demanded. "What have I done? Why did you kick me? What is your problem?" His voice got louder each time as he demanded to know why he was being maltreated.

"You'll know soon enough," Officer O'Connor promised as he forced Simeon down a flight of stairs that led into a basement with a long and isolated hallway with shiny floor.

"You think you're some hot shit!" Officer O'Connor said to Simeon as he pushed him down the hallway, calling him lousy scum.

"I need to make a call now. I have the right to a lawyer. I need to let my parents know where I am. I need my phone call now, sir. What have I done? What is my crime?" Simeon kept on.

Halfway into the long, lonely hallway void of doors and windows, Officer O'Connor unleashed his fury on Simeon. With his back pushed against the wall, he delivered his first punch in Simeon's stomach, pulled him by the shoulder, sank his right knee into his stomach, and continued to beat him mercilessly.

With a bloody face and battered body, Simeon continued to cry out for help. It did not matter how much or how loud he cried out, the sound of his voice could not travel beyond the basement. The assault continued unabated, and Simeon would probably not have survived had an employee of the police department not walked into the basement unexpectedly.

Rachel Epstein was on her way to the department's archive repository when she ran into them. Initially, she thought they were just fighting; but as she got closer, she noticed that one of the two had his hands cuffed behind his back. She came to a stop right next to them as Simeon was asking for help.

"Please help me. Help me, please," he cried out as Rachel Epstein stood there frozen with bewilderment and utter confusion.

She did not hear when Officer O'Connor ordered her to move on. She was jolted into consciousness once again when he shouted right in her face with some mixture of his saliva and sweat on her skin. "Move on!" he yelled as he pointed down the hallway.

Rachel, however, ran the other way, back toward the direction she had come—upstairs. She was still shaking in her office when she heard a knock on the door. "Who is it?" she asked.

"O'Connor. Open the door."

"What can I do for you?" she asked.

"Open the damn door and I'll tell you," he demanded in a less threatening voice.

"No sir, I will not."

"Well, then. I just wanted to explain to you that what you saw down in the basement wasn't quite what it seemed. I was the one assaulted by the suspect. He and his gang members are the prime suspects for the murder of Officer Nelson over the weekend. I just want you to keep whatever you think you saw down there to yourself. I hope we can understand each other. For all it's worth, I just wanted to make sure we understand one another."

Officer Nelson was found dead in his police car the same morning he and his colleagues went into Simeon's apartment to end their party. From what was available in the newspapers, the patrol car he was found in had no evidence of a struggle, considering that he was found with a string of his own intestine tied around his head, covering his nostrils and some of it stuffed in his mouth. What had the city in uproar was not so much his death, but more of the condition in which he was found. The butchery aspect of some of the recent deaths had the city and its surroundings on edge. It was for his death that Simeon and his friends were rounded up, although there was absence of any single evidence that connected them to the death.

*****

While Officer O'Connor was grooming himself for the evening, he told his wife he needed to go back to the office to finish a report he was working on regarding the death of Officer Nelson. He deposited a black duffle bag into his car and left wearing his police uniform. On his way out, he made a call from his car. "Hey, what are you wearing tonight, by the way?" He queried.

"I'll dress normally, but I'll have your favorite naughty red lingerie in the bag," Kimberly Ferguson responded.

"Make the underwear black," he recommended as he slipped a piece of gum into his mouth with his tongue receiving it as if it was a piece of the famous Holy Communion from a Catholic service. "Listen, I need to tidy up something at the office. I'll meet up with you at the grocery store in about forty-five minutes."

When he showed up at the grocery store parking lot to meet up with Ms. Ferguson, he parked his car beside hers, got out, and went into the store. She then drove to a different side of the store, parked her car, and entered through a different entrance. Officer O'Connor went through the store, not making any stop or eye contact and exited just a few minutes after Ms. Ferguson had entered and went straight to her car, opened the front door, and sunk himself in the front passenger seat. A few minutes later, she came back to her car and got on the driver's seat.

"I need you to go back in there and get me some Band-Aid or something."

"What happened to your face?" she asked as she looked at his scarred face.

"I cut myself shaving."

"Gosh, it looks like a fresh wound. It's still bleeding. You mean to tell me you did all that to yourself just from shaving? You need to stop the bleeding. Why are you so sweaty? If I hadn't seen you get here in your car, I would have thought you jogged your way through. I'll be right back."

"And a bottle of cold water too," he added just as she exited the car.

While Ms. Ferguson throttled down the street, Officer O'Connor wetted a stash of napkins he retrieved from the glove compartment and wiped off his sweaty face.

At the city jail where Simeon was left wondering his fate, he managed to clean himself up. And while he lay down, wishing he could endow himself with some supernatural feats, he felt his heart beating more and more rapidly to the extent that it became audible to him. The more he thought about revenge, the thirstier he got until he could no longer help but put his mouth to the sink in his cell. This time, the more he drank, the more he felt the tattoo symbol on his leg throbbing. The next thing he would remember later was being out of breath by the time he staggered to bed and laid down for a deep sleep.

At 1431 Ethan Drive, the fire department has just alerted the local police following the discovery of a body when they forced their way into a residence. A close neighbor had called the fire department when she noticed what was described as an unusual level of smoke coming from the residence. The police and the accompanying detectives were quick to realize that they were at the residence of one of the department's employees. The fire department had briefed the police that the smoke was due to a large amount of water from the pot of food that seemed overturned onto the burning gas stove. They added that the body of a woman under the cover was already dead by the time they got there.

The police quickly went in to examine the body; it was Rachael Epstein. Her body is covered with bruises, and the kitchen where her body was found bore the marks of severe struggle. Closer examination by the detectives revealed three of her right fingers were severed and nowhere to be found. Further examination by the detectives brought to light some substance under one of her two remaining fingernails: some dirt that the police were not immediately sure whether it came from the cooking pots and pans that were all over the floor.

"We're going to go ahead and turn it over to you guys and head on out of here. If it means anything," the fire captain continued, "the smoke alarms were all blaring when we got here. They only went off as the smoke cleared up."

"Thank you, sir, for that information," Detective Mohan responded as he prepared to guide the firefighters out.

Detective Mohan was called to the back of the building as he was trying to seal off the area he considered an area of interest. Behind the building, one of Rachael Epstein's missing fingers lay on the ground. Detective Mohan ordered it secured into a plastic bag and transported immediately to the lab for preservation, hoping that what he noticed under the fingernail might reveal something about the perpetrator.

Simeon was no longer just walking through the dusty path as he recalled in his prior "dreams." He levitated to the usual corner on the roadside where the blind man and a headless falcon camped, a place he now termed the oracle.

On both sides of the path as he levitated toward the oracle were people he assumed to be tall and bearded men. There were little children as well. The women were dressed like nuns with dresses that covered their entire bodies from their heads to their toes. He was not able to make any eye contact, and none of the people looked in his direction.

As he came to a stop before the oracle, all the birds on the surrounding trees wailed in panic and left their positions en masse. The hand of the blind man clutched something that looked like the Catholic rosary. He turned his head toward Simeon's position as if he were looking at him where he stood. He maintained the same position as if he were staring dead straight at him.

Simeon noticed that the mini cyclone he had become familiar with now had a resident owl that was spinning the other direction as the cyclone turned counterclockwise with some cloud of dust spilling off on its sides, then being absorbed into the body again. The owl had stopped with its face in the direction of Simeon. There was no evidence that it had any eye, yet it seemed to be staring at him.

As the blind man and the eyeless owl maintained their seeming gaze toward Simeon, an area of the ground opened up to reveal what seemed like a pot made of mud or clay, spewing some frozen gas. The frozen gas was quickly followed by a stream of water pouring out that only became more intense, but the ground around the pot remained as dry as the rest of the surrounding.

Then the water quickly solidified, rising as if someone was under the pot, raising it up until it turned into a mirror with a level of clarity that none had ever known to exist. Where the mirror stood was the same spot Simeon had maintained his gaze since he stopped. The mirror revealed him, but what he saw was not him. He kept looking at the mirror while the owl and the blind man kept their gazes at his direction, and the headless falcon continued to circle the mini cyclone.

Kim Ferguson and Officer O'Connor had checked into one of the suites in a secluded time-share resort that he often spent time with women he was able to win over, sometimes with promises of special favors or outright intimidation embedded with threats. The last time they were there, they arrived on a Friday evening, just like today, and did not leave until Monday evening, the end of a public holiday. Officer O'Connor had told his wife that he was attending a law enforcement seminar that would last until the holiday.

This evening, however, the officer is not having the best of time. He appeared troubled, sweating profusely, and could not seem to stop the gash in his face from bleeding. He threw his weight hard on the bed as soon as they walked in, letting out a long sigh. The facility, irrespective of being located in the secluded foothills of aesthetic mountains, had a decent security apparatus, and so time-sharing holders had never had to worry.

Rumors had swirled around for quite some time about the place. Popularly known as the Deep Ranch, it is where some of the country's top politicians rendezvous with their mistresses and high-class, highly paid prostitutes—otherwise lightly called escorts. It has also been the place where some notables that are still in the closet about their sexual orientation go to live their true selves beyond the eyes of many.

When Kim Ferguson stepped outside just minutes after they checked themselves in, she had no worry about any security shortcomings; after all, she knew that the man she came with always carried a gun. Indeed, Officer O'Connor had a gun with him just as he had always done in the past. Moreover, she would never accept that any attempt to breach the tranquility of the Deep Ranch would gain a foot of success. The security detail had never had an emergency in their functional aspect, and any anticipation of an anomaly is out of the question.

As Kim turned around to head back inside, having retrieved the cell phone she rested in the cup holder of her vehicle, an owl landed right in the middle of the top of the stairway leading to their suite. This was not just any owl. To Kim, it seemed more than twenty times the normal size of any owl she had ever seen in any zoo or television. However, that was not what startled her out of her sanity. The bird stretched its neck some two feet forward, curled it back, and the head went on a slow 360-degree continuous turn.

For what seemed like eternity to her, Kim remained frozen, standing there unaware of even her own existence. When she realized there was still some life left in her, she dashed back into her car and quickly locked the door. When a surge of comfort and sanity returned to her senses, she normalized. She quickly put her fingers to the phone, knowing that her officer companion was just across those same stairs with a loaded gun.

The phone rang, rang, and rang, but Officer O'Connor did not answer. She hung up, tried again and again, but there was no response. A swirl of panic ran down her neck and down to her tail bone. She thought about putting her hands heavily on the horn, but the last thing she wanted was to attract the attention of others.

As she raised her head to look at the owl again, there was nothing there. She looked to the left, but there was nothing there; to the right and all around the car, but there was no sign of the bird. She started the car, backed up, then forward—no sign of the bird. She cautiously opened the car door and came out. With shaky hands and a heart pounding so loudly that it was audible enough that she could hear her own heartbeat, she inspected her surroundings, and all was calm. She leaped over the stairs without knowing how she managed to do so, busted through the door, and slammed it shut past her instantly.

While she has managed to get inside the suite, her mood transitioned from that of being scared to anger and disappointment. "Why didn't he answer the damn phone? Why the hell did he not come out to see if I was all right all this while?"

Within a short interval, her brain processed a huge deal of information and she was ready to offload them on Officer O'Connor as she headed directly to the bedroom. She was already spitting and shooting out curses and swearing as she turned the corner to the bedroom, the only bedroom in the suite where the officer was when she left to retrieve her cell phone. However, what caught her sight as she looked on the bed consumed what consciousness and strength she had left. She passed out and fell helplessly onto the richly carpeted floor.

Detectives Mohan and Delaney had barely finished securing the Epstein's crime scene when they received a call: "Come to the Deep Ranch, stat. A body's been found." They quickly tidied up and headed for Deep Ranch, having requested that the headquarters dispatch a different crime scene mobile lab to the Ranch.

Deep Ranch had a different jurisdiction until recently when it was annexed by the city of Melyena, bringing it into its law enforcement jurisdiction.

Kim Ferguson ran out of the room when she regained consciousness. She had alerted the Deep Ranch security of the situation in building 67, the building that housed the suite she and Officer O'Connor checked into. Keeping their relationship a secret has just come to its end; the secrecy had run its course.

Detectives Delaney and Mohan were taken to the suite upon their arrival and shown the scene, which, at the time, had not been classified as that of a crime. When the detectives came into the room, they noticed a partially decapitated body of a male. The scene had no similarity to anything they had processed in the history of their profession nor had any of them heard of such a scene.

Detective Delaney tasked the crime scene photographer, "I want you to photograph everything. Do not touch anything whatsoever except to photograph everything, every corner, including the ceiling, windows, and curtains as you see them, the inside as well as the outside of the doors, windows, and ceilings, even the stairs. For Pete's sake, do not touch anything. I want to have a chat with the lady."

"Ms. Ferguson, would you like something to drink, some water or soda?" he asked as she sat motionless with both legs curled up and knees up to her chin.

She shook her head and then said no.

"Do you smoke? Want a cigarette?

She shook her head.

"Do you work here, ma'am?"

"No sir."

"I need to know what happened. Do you have an id? Can you help me with some information, perhaps by telling me how you got here and who the man in the bed is?"

"He was one of you. O'Connor. Jake O'Connor," she relayed.

"What do you mean?"

"What?" Who? Which Jake?" Are you saying it's Officer O'Connor's body lying in that bed?"

"Yes."

"How…what—"

"We come here from time to time," she interrupted and still with both feet curled up.

"Excuse me." Detective Delaney got up and went back to the suite. As he walked, he started thinking about O'Connor, *He was larger-than-life. He would bully his way in and out of every situation, almost every situation. What in God's name could it be that has now rendered him to a mere carcass?*

"I was just coming to join you there," Detective Mohan said, interrupting Delaney's thoughts. "It looks like we've got our work cut out for us, doesn't it?"

"What an understatement," Delaney murmured under his breath.

"Care to guess who it is lying on that bed?"

"How the hell would I know. I haven't touched anything."

Standing right in the room, right next to the bed, Detective Delaney turned to Detective Mohan and said, "This is Officer O'Connor," as he pointed to the body, or what was left of him lying on his back in the middle of the bed.

The two eye sockets were empty, each socket resembled something that was surgically carved around and the eyeball removed. Around each socket looked like there was a controlled, smooth burn. The upper lip was cut out right below the nose, and the flesh was removed. The lower lip was cut out right above the chin, leaving the upper and lower set of teeth bare and exposed. The left and right knuckles were completely crushed along with the outer skin. His pants and underwear were down to his knees with both shoes on his feet undisturbed. All around his pelvis, the skin seemed to have been surgically excised, exposing his penis and testicles, but the skin was nowhere to be found.

The facility security had informed the detectives that there was still some muscle twitching around the pelvic area when they first came into the room, that his testicles were still twitching. There was not a drop of blood anywhere. The detectives and the rest of the crime scene personnel present were speechless.

One of the female crime scene processors that once had a nine-month fling with the now-deceased officer, upon learning it was him—or what was left of him lying there—ran outside and threw up, coating the well-manicured lawn with what she had for dinner.

Perhaps still in disbelief that the body lying there was that of Officer O'Connor, Detective Mohan ordered that O'Connor's fingerprint be taken immediately, adding, "And I needed that confirmed yesterday." He was already informed that the gash on the left side of his face resulted from a shaving mishap, and that it was still bleeding when they met up that evening. Detective Mohan then requested that someone from the investigative unit be dispatched to the grocery store for the possibility of securing all available video records.

Simeon woke up with worries about what he termed another episode of unusual nightmares. His hands were over his face, his ears, and his head as he headed directly to his bathroom for a look in the mirror. "God damn it. My God! What the freaking hell was that?" he exclaimed as he made his way.

He was relieved to see there was nothing out of his usual appearance. He had not become the image he tattooed on his leg, nor had he grown rabbit ears. What he saw in the liquid mirror was a Simeon that was taken over by his tattoo character. A figure that has taken over its host, altered his physical appearance and imposed on him some uncanny characteristics. "What a nightmare!" he muttered.

He stood there for a while, wondering what that "dream" was all about. He was delighted in the aesthetics of the liquid mirror. The manner that water and gas bubbled up to form a mirror with utmost clarity, revealing what he thought was himself but under a curse, demonized, and disfigured. When he looked into the liquid mirror, what he saw was the symbol or character he tattooed on his leg; he saw Zeus.

Irrespective of whatever narratives Kim Ferguson had given to the detectives, they put the cuffs on her, put her in the squad car, and took her with them. Not even for a second did her story make any sense to them. All they concluded was that Ms. Ferguson was squarely in the midst of whatever took place that resulted in the death of the person whose body they found there. As far as they were concerned, she was yet to tell them what happened or what she knew about all the events that took place.

Upon their arrival at the station, Detectives Delaney and Mohan were summoned to report immediately to the crime lab. "Detectives Delaney…Mohan, please come with me," the messenger requested. When they settled on the basement three floors below ground level, they were told that the fingers found in a duffle bag in the trunk of Officer O'Connor's car belonged to Rachel Epstein. The detectives looked at each other, and then looked steadily at the lab technician that delivered the message. They stood there silently.

"Officer O'Connor is dead. The only one we have that can shed any light on this whole mess is that Ferguson woman," Detective Mohan managed to say.

They left to attend an impromptu meeting just before a news release.

During their meeting there was a consensus on how quickly Officer O'Connor's wife had to be notified. A female officer was chosen to deliver the news, accompanied by two male officers and a driver that was instructed to remain with the vehicle and act like a professional chauffeur to the female officer. The appointees groomed themselves for the task and were on their way to Officer O'Connor's residence in short notice.

No matter how hard Mrs. O'Connor demanded and pushed for the details on how her husband died, Officer Rebecca O'Keefe calmly replied, "The details are not yet available. Every available hand in the entire force is busy trying to sort things out. You have to understand that this is a priority for the force, and I understand how important it is for you to have some answers. Unfortunately, those answers that we're all eager to have are indeed not yet available. I can only promise you that we'll get them, and once we're able to tie things together, you'll be the first to know. I promise."

It was barely seven hours after Mrs. Edna O'Connor was officially informed of her husband's death when she heard of someone being held for questioning. She was at her house with her parents, some of her siblings, and friends who came to offer some support. As she was there with those that for the most part amounted to a support group, the television paused its normal program to deliver what it called "breaking news." The reporter went on to say, "A woman whom the police said was Officer O'Connor's lover is being held for questioning after she was picked up from the Deep Ranch resort where she and the now-deceased officer both went for some rest and relaxation. Our source revealed that the woman's account of events to the police regarding what took place at Deep Ranch did not add up, and she was being held as the number one person of interest, perhaps the number one suspect.

"When asked what information provided by the woman that did not add up, the source revealed that the woman started talking about some headless bird that she encountered when she went to her car to retrieve her cell phone while Officer O'Connor was in the room alone. It's not only enough that her account of event is bizarre, but it more than anything else casts some doubt as to her sanity."

On hearing the news brief, Mrs. O'Connor went into her bedroom, her mother on her heels behind her just as the television was turned off. Resting both elbows on the base of a bedroom window with her palms over her face, she sobbed as her mother held her closely, her own tears running down her aging cheeks. She wiped off her tears, held her daughter closely as if she was trying to wrap her with her own body. She continued to kiss her on her head while stroking her hair, tears running down her cheeks as Edna continued to cry loudly.

"It'll be all right. It's a test in life. Life deals us with sadness, but that too shall pass. We just have to have faith. It'll be all right. I love you. It'll be all right," she continued as she gently rocked Edna from side to side.

Edna looked at her mother's teary face; they both hugged each other tightly. She wiped Edna's eyes, but she broke free and turned again toward the window to look in the direction of her two-year-old son playing in the backyard with his little cousins. A lot was going through her mind, although one might have thought she was looking at the children.

As she gazed through the window, not focused on anything in particular, three vultures descended simultaneously and abruptly close to the children, much like something that was choreographed. The scene heightened her attention. The birds took off just as abruptly as they landed. Edna was aware her heartbeat was faster and loud—she could actually hear it.

Then three birds landed again before she could even wrap her head on what just happened. This time, the birds, although they resembled vultures, had only about three feathers on the tip of each wing; and as soon as they landed, all three started walking toward the children in a synchronized manner. Having noticed the birds, the children walked toward them, talking as they walked.

"No, Nick. No, no. Nicholas," Edna shouted, forgetting that the window was closed.

"Mom," she shouted, calling her mother's attention.

Her mother, who had left for the bathroom, was already coming back when she heard Edna yelling. She rushed back in as Edna was opening the window.

As they both watched, the three vultures lined up and started moving in a tight circular formation. That was when they noticed that none of the vultures had a head, only necks from which blood dripped. As both remained frozen in shock and panic, the vultures leaped onto Edna's son, lifted little Nick as if he were a piece of paper, and took off with him.

"Mommy, mommy," little Nick called out repeatedly as the sight and sound of him waned before their eyes.

Edna's mother was left shouting as everyone in the house rushed into the room. Edna lay stretched out on the floor, motionless, unresponsive to the commotion in the room. She had fainted when her senses were overwhelmed by the events around her. Her knees became too weak to keep her upright on her feet the very moment consciousness exited. She fell.

While some people attended to what seemed like Edna's lifeless body, her mother was pointing outside, crying loudly, "Nick. They took Nick. They took my Nick, my little Nick. What is going on? God, what is going on? What is really going on?"

Those looking out from inside the room and the others that already made it out to the yard noticed that the children were all looking and pointing to the sky.

It did not take long before the wailing sirens engulfed the neighborhood. There were the loud unmistaken horns of the fire trucks blasting repeatedly. Everyone thought someone must have called the police. Amid the commotion, it did not occur to anyone to call 911 as everyone was running around trying to make some sense about what was going on.

Within a short time, it became clear that the sirens and horns were not coming closer to the O'Connor residence. In fact, whatever they were—the police, EMS, fire trucks, or all of them—were headed to a completely different direction. Even the media that were locked outside of the O'Connor gates quickly jumped into their vehicles to chase the sound of the sirens.

Most of them thought, *They are going the wrong direction.*

A young lady got on the phone and called 911 to alert them and perhaps give them the correct address. "Ma'am, the EMS is going the wrong way," she started. "The address is 9347 Esau Clove. My name is Janice. Please hurry. I don't think she's breathing."

"Who's not breathing?" the dispatcher queried.

"Mrs. O'Connor."

"What's wrong with her? Why is she not breathing?"

"She's not moving. Could you please give the correct address to the ambulance?"

"I will send an ambulance. You said the address was 9347 Esau—"

"Yes, ma'am. I still hear their siren, but they seem to be going farther away. If you could just give them the correct address."

"Sorry, ma'am, but we did not get any call for this address. You're not calling for the child that was up in the lighthouse tower, are you?"

"What?"

"Ambulance is on its way. Stay on the phone with me, will you?"

"Yes."

The dispatcher lost Janice's attention the moment she mentioned a child up in the lighthouse tower. She had hung up the phone barely after she said yes as she immediately imagined little Nick, her first cousin, crying up there all alone. She imagined what must be going through his mind. The torment, agony, his psychological state—he's just a child. "She said something about a child on the lighthouse tower," she told other family members right before she busted into tears. She then secluded herself to a corner, bent over, her right hand clutching her stomach as she cried deeply.

The gates were wide open for the ambulance as it made its way into the compound while some of the people quickly left, running toward the direction of the lighthouse. The old harbor where the lighthouse was located became a landing zone for spectators. It was buzzing with people of varying interests. Those on the ground, despite the noise they generate, could hear the crying of a child coming from the thin, narrow tower that hosts a large wind vane on its very top. The abandoned light house has stood there for many years since it became replaced by newer, more reliable navigational technology. Its presence only serves as a relic; a reminder of what was.

The firemen had decided to extend their layers of ladders straight to the tower, having concluded it would take unreasonably too long to breach the one steel door that gave access to several flights of stairs to the top. They extended their ladders with two men and harnesses properly and surely secured. The end of the ladder rested on the wall of the tower, making it more reassuring. It was, indeed, little Nick.

The firefighter that had breached the partition between two little holes gave a hand signal that all was well. The other rescue person would now descend using the sliding device just as they rehearsed. The firefighters wanted to eliminate every chance of exerting excessive weight on the ladder, although they had carried out numerous dry runs with three adults on the ladder simulating a scenario, not exactly but similar to present condition. He signaled to the ground unit that he was coming down; they, in turn, gave their go-ahead, and the man let go of the ladder. He was stabilized on the ground in a blink of an eye.

It was now time to home the ladder and complete the rescue. They would start retracting as soon as they get the go-ahead from the only rescue person left on the ladder. He gave a hand signal for the ground crew to commence retraction. The ladder had cleared about five feet away from the wall when the firefighter turned his face to their direction as he held little Nick firmly and securely in his grasp.

"Who the hell is that?" the retraction mechanism operator asked loudly when he noticed that the rescuer was not the same person they sent up there. In a reflex, he stopped the retraction process.

The question that was on the mind of every member of the fire team was "Who is that?"—and some said it aloud.

"Sergeant Manning, what the hell happened up there?" Sergeant Manning was the other person that was up there that came back using the sliding mechanism.

"Sir, I do not have a different answer for you. I wish I did. What you are seeing is also what I am seeing."

Those that gathered to see the rescue operation, the ones that saw the two men go up on the ladder, knew that the person holding the child was not the same person they saw going up. To some of them, the face sure looked familiar while some immediately recognized him.

"Well, retract the ladder. Let's see. After all, he still has the child," the sergeant advised.

"Keep your guards up, guys," the deputy fire marshal cautioned while he stepped up to the retraction switch area. "I'll take it from here." He sank his right thumb into the hole and depressed the retraction switch. But as soon as he pushed it, the entire ladder assembly detached from the harness on the fire truck, falling heavily onto the concrete pavement with force that seemed as if other forces accelerated its descent and with added momentum. It burst into flames where the end made contact with the concrete pavement, leaving some eight-foot crater colored with black smoke residue.

A huge cloud of white smoke had initially engulfed the area for a short time when it hit the ground, but it quickly transformed into a much larger cloud of black smoke as those that were present watched. The rescue unit, the ambulance, the police, and everyone else present, all were astonished as to why there was any fire at all when the ladder fell. One might have been able to explain a spark as something plausible, but fire was beyond everyone's realm of rationality. There was no fuel source to account for the burning. Everyone was horrified as the ladder made its ferocious descent.

"Oh! no!"

"Oh! My god"

"Jesus Christ."

"God, no!"

"Oh shit!"

The crowd could not contain themselves about the words or phrases they used to express their surprise. Maybe what they just witnessed was too hard to swallow, or that they deemed it somewhat impossible to accept as a present reality and an actual occurrence.

There were people crying. Some had their hands over their mouths. Some had their mouths wide open as if they had some questions they were unable to ask. Many stood dumbfounded, not sure whether they had just had a nightmare or whether the end-time had come upon them.

News had started circulating: "Mrs. O'Connor did not make it. His mother has passed. The coroner had come to pick up a charred body of a little child."

What a way to die, some were murmuring to themselves.

"What a sight for a mother to see her child taken like that. Just taken in broad daylight," a spectator murmured.

There were now pockets or groups of the spectators. In small groups of a few, they were talking freely behind the cordoned off-area. "Remember that guy that was charged for a gruesome murder? They said he ripped the internal organs of his victim, remember?

That person holding the baby looked like him," one person said to her group of three individuals.

"Yes, I remember him. Didn't they also pick him up for killing a police officer not long ago?"

"Exactly. If that wasn't him, it sure as hell looked like him."

It did not take long before a name was being tossed around. "That definitely looked like Simeon Rhenoake. He sure did."

The police at the scene had themselves confirmed that Simeon was still in police custody, still in the cell that Officer O'Connor put him.

On the evening news were videos of the rescue, the many shots and angles of it. The shots of the person holding the child revealed it was indeed Simeon Rhenoake. When the ladder hit the concrete pavement and busted into flames, not one of the people present saw anything other than the cloud of white smoke that was overtaken by black cloud. However, every video shown on the evening news had a bird flying away from the cloud of smoke, but no one could account for where it might have come from.

The investigation as to the whereabouts of Mr. Simeon Rhenoake at the very moment of the rescue did not take long to conclude he was indeed in his cell. The authorities were becoming nervous about confronting him. It seemed they had come to accept that Simeon was out for revenge since Rachael Epstein, before her death, confided in a friend about Simeon's assault in the hands of Officer O'Connor. Ms. Epstein's confidant relayed to the authorities that she had told her of the Officer's threat should she share her encounter with anyone. The information she shared with them helped the police conclude with confidence that Epstein died at the hands of O'Connor.

When it came up that they needed to have a talk with Simeon, no one volunteered. Three detectives were ultimately assigned to be present in the room where he was brought to answer some questions. Many more monitored through cameras, ready to spring into action should the need arise. The three officers in the room were nervous as hell, although they did their best to put a bold face. "Can I call you Simeon?" Detective Sheehan started.

"That's my name."

"Okay, Simeon, my name is David Sheehan. You can call me David—"

"Listen," Simeon interrupted, "all I want to know is why I am being kept here. If I have committed a crime, then charge me and bring your evidence. I am asking for justice."

"That is exactly what we're here for, Simeon, to seek justice. Do you think that what happened to Nick O'Connor served any justice?"

"Are you asking me, David? Are you asking me?" Simeon responded. "Do you think that shooting and killing an unarmed man is justice, David, leaving his son fatherless, leaving his wife without a husband? Do you think that making the wife's life ten times as hard to provide for the child is justice, David? You want to lecture me about justice? You split-tongued serpent, do you really want to spew your justice rhetoric to me? Tell me, then, what exactly is the dead man's child guilty of? What exactly is the dead man's wife guilty of?"

Simeon's skin was visibly beginning to turn somewhat purple. Then he got up. All the three detectives startled as he did so, with Detective Sheehan visibly more nervous. A few years ago, he had shot and killed an unarmed man. His excuse was that he thought his victim might have a gun that he could have used to shoot him. Fortunately for him and his like, his victim belonged to the group whose lives never mattered much and who never dared lift a finger to fight back. So they simply bury their dead, sing some idiotic songs, and prepare their children to sing the same song in the years to come because their mental capacity to reason is severely retarded. Their only act of bravery has always been to die in their misplaced urge to please their masters in every battle from which they stand to gain nothing other than more hatred and diminished human worth.

"I need some water," Simeon requested.

"Simeon, calm down"

"I need some water to drink. Would it be justice for your kids to get the same justice you accord other's kids, David?"

He turned to the other two that have so far remained spectators and asked, "How about you two? Want to trade places?"

"I'll get you some water, Simeon?" Detective Holmes volunteered as he got up and exited the room. The more they looked at Simeon, the more they realized that his face was beginning to take the shape of the tattoo on his leg. They noticed his chest pump in and out with each heartbeat.

Afraid of using a glass, Holmes brought the water in a plastic cup. "We don't have glasses here" he softly uttered in an apologetic voice.

Simeon gulped down the water, looked at Detective Holmes for a few seconds, and then laid the cup on the table in front of him. "I do not need anything from you, and I don't have anything to give you." He sat back down and laid his head on the table.

The detectives looked at each other. "Let's take you back to your cell, Simeon," Sheehan offered.

The three detectives stood outside Simeon's cell to see the metal door slide completely shut. From the other side, Simeon turned and gazed at detective Sheehan for a few minutes without blinking, and then he turned and walked to his bed. The look on his face had detective Sheehan unsettled. He was worried, but he couldn't quite wrap his head around his uneasiness.

He called his wife while seated at his desk. He just wanted to talk to someone—anyone—that has nothing to do with his work or his type of work. They had both agreed to leave work matters where they belong—at work.

On the day he shot and killed an unarmed man, he called his wife to let her know what had happened. "Listen, I just wanted to let you know before you have to hear it from the media. In the course of my work today, I had to fire a shot to safeguard my life, and the suspect expired. The subject was black," he advised his wife. At home that very day, his wife advised him that she did not want to hear the details about the incident, adding that she did not want to deal with the distraction. Every time it came on the news, his wife would change the station. She had continued her life resigned to never know or discuss the details of the incident, and so those details, whatever they were, remained unknown to her.

The St. Patrick Catholic Church could not contain all the people that came to pay their respects to the O'Connor family. Many people were outside the church, braving the frigid drizzling weather. One service was held for Officer O'Connor, his wife, and his son, and the three coffins were laid there in front of the altar as Father O'Keefe performed the requiem.

As the reverend passed the incense from one coffin to the other, a bird suddenly landed on the base of one of the upper stained-glass windows in the church, prompting a chaotic exodus of some of those inside the church to the outside. It was an owl, an unusually huge owl with unusually huge wings, swaying from side to side as it sat there looking toward the altar.

As the crowd in the church forced their way to the outside, Father O'Keefe ignored the commotion, raising his voice even louder as he went on with his incantations. He turned to the direction of the owl, raised the incense, waved it three times in the same direction, lowered it, then raised it, and waved three times again; he did so three times as he loudly rebuked evil spirits. "This is the house of God, cleansed with the blood of Jesus. No evil can stain it," he said.

The owl hopped up to the top opening from where it came, put its head to the outside, and flew away. As people watched it flap its huge wings and disappeared, a wave of even colder and seemingly dead air passed through the congregation. It was so strong that it blew off some of the candles in the church. People looked at each other without uttering a word. Many kept kissing their rosaries while others repeatedly made the sign of the cross. "There must not be darkness in the house of God. There must not be darkness," Father O'Keefe said as he handed the incense to an altar boy, then went around and lit every candle that was blown off.

Many people attended the burial of the O'Connors despite the frigid rain at the Irish cemetery where they were laid to rest, three of them buried next to each other with their child in the middle. The cemetery was full, and those that could not fit in the immediate area stayed at nearby streets, hurdled under umbrellas. People were uneasy and jumped at the sight of any bird.

Simeon was kept under surveillance in his cell to ascertain his presence there. As far as the surveillance team was concerned, Simeon was in his bed sleeping and his cell locked and secured.

It rained heavily the night after the burial. It was as if the heavens opened and emptied everything it had. When the day came, the city authorities were flooded with calls reporting an unearthed grave and a casket sitting on top of the ground. When the city officials responded, they noticed that the casket in which Officer O'Connor was buried lay on top of what was the grave in which he was buried. It was open with no corpse inside. It was as if someone or something dug up the grave, brought out the casket, covered up the grave with dirt, and laid the casket on the top of it. The men, who were shortly joined by some police officers, went around the cemetery looking to find the corpse that should have been in the casket but could not locate it.

As detective Sheehan sat at the dinner table with his wife and their seventeen-year-old son, he noticed that his son seemed somewhat distant. He could not help but notice that he ate his meal with some hesitation and displayed an unusual lack of interest. The manner in which he gazed at his plate gave away his preoccupation with something. "May I ask what the problem is?" Detective Sheehan asked. "Lack of appetite or just don't like the food? Is there something else you'd rather be eating?"

"Dad, remember that guy that was on TV a few days ago? The one they said was supposed to be in jail but somehow showed up as a fireman to rescue the little boy?" Daniel asked, not addressing directly what his father had asked about the food and his seeming preoccupation.

The question immediately caught the detective's attention. He swallowed what was in his mouth, lowered his fork, and rested it on the plate while looking up directly at his son. "What about him?" he demanded with a more rapid heartbeat and a louder voice.

"This morning when I pulled into the parking lot at school, there was this guy standing by the flag pole looking and smiling at me. He looked just like him. And when it was time to come home, I saw him standing on one end of the crosswalk, again looking and smiling at me. However, what was strange is that other people crossing the driveway did not appear to see him. It seemed people just walked through him, as if he was not there. They went about their businesses in a manner that showed that either he was not there or that he was totally invisible, and they walked into him and exited.

"I do not know if it's my mind playing tricks on me because when I pulled up in our driveway, I caught a glimpse of him in the rearview mirror standing behind my car, but he was not there when I got out. I walked and searched around the car, but there was no sight of him. I thought that was strange."

Whatever appetite detective Sheehan had earlier evaporated the very moment his son started telling him what he experienced. The taste in his mouth was no longer that of the food he was eating. His heart was racing, and his brain was processing millions of incoherent pieces of information per second. His wife sat there speechless, interchanging her stare between her husband and her son.

He stood up, paced the floor for a few minutes, then went to the front window of his house and peered outside as if to make sure no one was there. He went back to his son. "So, as far as you know, you didn't think anyone else saw him?"

"No, it didn't seem like anyone else noticed him. Maybe it's my mind playing tricks on me but I—"

"No, you're fine, Dan. Your mind was not playing any trick on you. There's sure some evil going on with that guy. I only wish I knew what it is or how to put an end to it. Eat your food. Over my dead body would I let anything happen to you or any member of this family."

He left to check that all the doors leading to the outside were locked, then went into his room to ensure that his guns were still where he left them. He inspected all the rooms in his house to reassure himself that things were orderly. He reassured himself he would not make any silly mistake.

When calls came into Melyena City officials that someone had committed suicide on the overpass of a major intersection, firefighters were immediately dispatched. As they approached, the team noticed that a body was indeed hanging over the street below from the base of a streetlight on the overpass. The body was dressed in a police uniform, and the face of the person was partially gone. It did not take them time to digest that it was the body of Officer O'Connor that was mysteriously unearthed from the grave the night after he was buried. They put a plastic cover over his face and lowered the body as onlookers watched. Among the police, the coroner's office, and the firefighters, a body bag was produced, and the body was put into the bag and hauled away in a van.

"This has got to be the last insult," a fireman said as they talked among themselves.

The next day, one of the local newspapers had the caption: "Revenge or Ultimate Insult?" Below the caption was a picture of Officer O'Connor taken the day he graduated from the police academy. Two days later, he was entombed in the same grave next to his son with heavy concrete slabs laid over the three graves.

Detective Sheehan decided he could not simply go to sleep with the level of uneasiness that had enveloped him. He decided to drive to the city jail and visit Simeon. On arrival, he looked into his cell, and then headed for the warden's station when he saw him coming out of the men's room. "Where is he this time of the night?" he asked the warden.

"Where's who?"

"Simeon Rhenoake."

"You mean our strange resident? He's in there in his cell."

"No, he's not. I just came from there."

"I looked in the monitor just a minute ago, and he was there."

They both quickly walked to his station. "See, there he is. You had me worried there for a minute."

"I came to you because he wasn't there when I checked his cell just a minute ago."

"Come with me and let's take a look, will ya?" the warden asked the detective as he headed toward Simeon's cell.

As they both stood in front of the steel door of the cell, the warden pointed to the inside where Simeon was on the bed presumed asleep. Detective Sheehan was sure that Simeon was not there in that cell when he came in; however, he did not want to adamantly emphasize it to the warden. He thought his sanity might be called into question if he did. "I just came to check on something. I'll go home now. Have a good night, sir."

"You've got to get a grip of yourself, Detective," The jail warden verbally appended.

Detective Sheehan headed toward the wide, long flight of stairs that led from the front of the jailhouse to the street. There was a male figure at the front of the stairs leaning on the guardrail with his back to the detective. As the detective got closer, the male figure turned his head in his direction.

Detective Sheehan almost fell down the stairs as he lost his coordination when he noticed that the person standing in front of him was Simeon. A bit of the thoughts in his head came aloud when he said, "That can't be," noting that Simeon was just in his cell back inside the building. He quickly looked behind him out of reflex, but there was no one there. When he turned again, Simeon was gone. He looked around but could not see any sign of him. He began to sweat. His heartbeat became a bit louder and his pulse slightly faster. He made sure there was no one in his car before he got in and sped home.

When he pulled his car into the garage in his home, he chambered a bullet in the gun he had with him before getting out of the vehicle. He could no longer trust his surroundings. In his mind, Simeon could be anywhere, and he was determined to fire should he appear anywhere around his house. He tucked the gun in between his jeans at his back and pulled down his jacket.

All was tranquil as he quietly shut the door of his car and headed inside. Just as he stretched his right hand to turn the doorknob that led into his house, he heard a door shut inside the house. He hesitated for a moment and then went inside, heading straight into the bedroom he shared with his wife. He observed his wife well asleep. He went to the room where his son slept only to see that he too was asleep. He quietly left the room and shut the door behind him.

He decided to check the two remaining rooms in the house. He drew his gun with a round already chambered. He quietly opened the third bedroom. He did not find anything unusual in the bedroom; however, he heard a noise he concluded was coming from the bedroom next to where he was. He turned off the safety switch of the gun and decided to get to the room through a shared bathroom, moving as quietly as he could. As he entered the room with his gun in a firing position, he noticed that the window at the back of the room was open and the blind dangling. The door leading from the bedroom into the hallway that led to the living room was open.

Noting that there was no one in the room, he quickly made his way to the door, then into the hallway, and as he looked through to the living room, he saw a figure heading toward his son's room. He realized that the clothing resembled the same blue and yellow colors Simeon was wearing when he saw him a while earlier. He did not hesitate to act. *It's now or never. It is my house and there is nowhere to run to,* he thought. He leveled his gun against "Simeon" and sank in three shots into the back of his head and neck.

The sound of the shots was too loud for Mrs. Sheehan to sleep through. She ran into the living room half naked. "What happened?" she asked her husband as he stood, still clutching the gun. She quickly ran to the body on the floor, defying her husband who motioned her not to move.

Kneeling next to the body while she called, "Daniel, Daniel," Theresa Sheehan turned the body face up and pulled him against her body, clutching him ever so tightly to herself and repeating his name as tears poured from her eyes, her mouth wide open. "What have you done, David? What have you done? You killed my son. You killed my son. You son of a bitch. You killed him."

Detective Sheehan stood there, gazing at them. Not a word, fixed without expression. From his standpoint, everything was in slow motion. His view was as if he was on a stage looking down on an act with a strange scene. He was unable to blink and could not hear the cries from his wife. It was as if he sustained some shell shock that gravely altered his senses. The more he looked at the two of them, the farther away they seemed from where he stood. The entire room was spinning around with him in the middle, watching it all.

After what seemed like eternity, Sheehan seemed relieved from whatever it was that had him transfixed. He heard his wife wail in hopeless agony. He turned, looked around the room, looked at the gun, looked at his wife holding their son—the tears in her eyes. He took one last look at the gun still clutched in his hand, put it at the right side of his head, and squeezed on the trigger. Detective Sheehan fell to his living room floor, dead before he hit the floor in a manner reminiscent of a banana tree chopped off from its base.

"Where's your new suit? Shouldn't you be wearing one for his funeral?" Simeon asked Mr. Wilmer, the jail warden, as they encountered each other in the hallway to his office. "Make sure it's a new one."

"How did you get here? I just left your cell. Who was in your bed? I mean, who let you out and just what—" Mr. Wilmer did not finish his sentence before a cold spell fell unto him. His speech slowed and his limbs froze for an instance. For the few seconds or so that he was under what seemed like a spell, he noticed that Simeon faded away as if he was just an apparition.

Mr. Wilmer slowly walked away in silence, not knowing what to make of the experience and the exchange he had. He shut his office door behind him, sat down, and quickly made a phone call to detective Sheehan, but his call immediately went to a voice mail. He put down the phone and wondered if what he just experienced actually happened or whether it was his senses playing tricks on him. He resolved to never share the experience with anyone.

It wasn't long before Warden Wilmer learned of Detective Sheehan's demise, the tragic nature of it, and the very fact that it all took place at his own house. It was the last thing he ever expected to hear in light of the fact that he was just with him less than two hours ago. As the news of the night's event circulated, he felt compelled to share the experience he had sworn to keep to himself.

When Mr. Wilmer relayed how detective Sheehan came to the department in the middle of the night and the only question he threw at him was the whereabouts of Simeon, it didn't seem that his audience made anything out of it. However, when he added that he ran into Simeon on his way to his office having confirmed him locked in his cell and asleep, his remarks about a new suit for a funeral, and his surprise that he could not tell how he made it out of a locked cell, Officer Pearle's attention was piqued.

It would be rare to find anyone in the department, perhaps in the wider city, who has not heard of Simeon. It did not take long before Officer Pearle was in the midst of a group of police officers with him as the main topic of discussion and suggestions as to what his fate ought to be, legal or otherwise, but to finally put an end to something a growing number of them saw as a menace. With their use of crafty means to cross legal hurdles, they have managed to keep him locked up longer than he ought to be.

As other officers saw the gathering of their "partners," they joined in on the ongoing conversation, and various scenaria were soon being floated for just a particular objective, legal or not. They became convinced that Simeon had something to do with the death of Sheehan and his son, although he was still behind bars while his friends who were picked up with him had long been released. The group dispersed as soon as the funeral procession ended.

When Sephinia Rhenoake could not get in contact with her son for what she thought was too long, she started calling some of his friends, trying to find out his whereabouts. She was not far off from her prediction that her son would not attempt to contact her even if he was in trouble. She had reluctantly pulled back on babying her son after his unflinching assertion that he has matured enough to be able to take care of himself. It was not something he achieved easily as his mother was always worried about him. It wasn't until he moved out of state that she finally succumbed to the idea of easing off.

When she divorced his father, Richard Rhenoake, and remarried, she never deviated from her routine of treating Simeon as if he was still a child. He often felt irritated to the point that he chose to spend more of his time with his friends rather than stay at home or be around his mother. As the only son of his mother, those around them knew that Simeon had his mother's full attention at all times, especially during the times that his father was away on military deployments. His upbringing was with his mother as they were never able to live together in any of the foreign countries where his father was deployed. Perhaps due to the nature of his assignments and the tasks he undertook, he was never able to be present in the lives of his wife and son. She thought that now that they have reunited in the same city once again, Simeon would no longer distance himself.

She was infuriated when she found out that her only son had been locked away in police custody for so long, and no one bothered to inform her. She had asked one of Simeon's friends to let her know if her son was ever in any trouble. Toward that objective, she gave Andrew her phone number and advised him to not let Simeon know. She encouraged him to not hesitate to call her should Simeon find himself in any kind of trouble.

As it went, Andy's loyalty to his friend proved to be more compelling than to abide by Sephinia's plea for secrecy. Upon telling Simeon, he advised Andy to lose the phone number, reminding him that they were "adults now" with no need for babysitters. Andy simply obliged.

Warden Wilmer was resting in his office, his forehead on the desk having just returned from Detective Sheehan's funeral. For just the few minutes he dozed off, he was walking through a cold winding alley. The plants and flowers seemed frozen without air. There was no wind from any direction. The only sound was his footsteps that echoed around him while everything else seemed frozen in time.

However, as he walked farther ahead, he heard what sounded like water dripping from a faucet. As he walked up to the source of the sound, he noticed an antique mailbox with a chair right next to it. Sitting on the chair was exactly the character of Simeon's tattoo holding a cup and water dripping from the mailbox into the cup.

As he stared at the scene, he saw the character raise its eyes toward him. Then he saw it blink. That was when he jolted himself awake. "Jesus! Son of a...," he murmured; and as he looked up, he saw Simeon standing across from his office. His pulse surged. He looked down at the top of his desk, then raised his head to look at him again; he was not there. He ran out and looked in both directions, but there was no sign of Simeon in either direction of the long and desolate hallway.

Sephinia Rhenoake stormed into the Melyena Police Department, having learned that her son was there. She demanded that someone explain to her the crime her son committed or the reason he was held there. She was adamant and refused to quiet down. Although she was intensely insistent she would not leave until she received an explanation, she briefly left when no one would respond to her any longer. But it did not take long before she returned. When she asked to see her son, the response was more courteous. "We'll get him for you in just a moment, ma'am. Will you please come with me?" a female officer requested as she led the way into a large room. "Wait right here, and I'll get him for you."

When Simeon walked into the room where his mother was waiting, he did not seem anxious or concerned. His demeanor was nothing like that of a son that has missed his mother because he was deprived of some level of freedom or right. He just quietly walked to her mother and sat down. The only thing he had to say was "Hi, mom," and he showed no expression.

Sephinia was dumbfounded when she saw him come into the room. He was not the son she knew; he wasn't that only son that she raised and known all along anymore. To her, he looked as if something had assumed her son's body and ravaged him from the inside out. "What have they done to you," she asked, running her hands from his head down to his shoulder.

He kept reassuring his mother that he was all right and not to worry. "I can handle the situation, Mom," he promised, adding that he was the one in control of the situation. "In the end, you'll see. I promise. My laugh is bound to be the last to come. I will bury all of them if I have to. Let's just hope it doesn't come to that."

The expression on his face as he made the statements startled his mother.

"Some have gone. Others may follow. Let them enjoy their false sense of invincibility for now, and I will make moths out of them when the time is ripe."

"I cannot say that I understand what you have just said, but I must say that you are scaring me, Simeon. I have been worried sick about you, and you did not even bother to attempt to contact me. Now that I have managed to find you, the reception has not been anything I would expect from my own son."

"I am sorry, Mom, if I seem unenthusiastic. I have remained here for several weeks now, and the experience has not been something I would consider a source of joy."

"I have talked to a lawyer. I did so as soon as I heard of your predicament, and he's hard at work putting together what he needs to mount a severe challenge to this kind of atrocity and cruelty that now prevails."

"No, Mom, I don't need a lawyer. I can fend for myself, and I intend to do so adequately. Tell your lawyer friend to stand down. Listen, Mom, it has come to that state where every man has to take a stand however he can and by whatever means he deems necessary for his own survival. History tells us that if you submit yourself to slavery, then you surely deserve whatever you get and would only have yourself to blame, not your master. I intend to stand as a man and would readily die doing so.

"To mortgage your sweat for a lawyer is to play their game just as they have written the script. No, I do not intend to play according to their script, on their own schedule, and at their venue. You have to leave now, Mom, before it gets dark. The night harbors a lot that are obscure to the common eyes. You must go now."

"Simeon, son, what has gotten into you? You sound as if you are in a war against the world. What have they done to you here?" Looking frustrated and worried at the same time, Sephinia maintained her searching eyes all around Simeon's face, occasionally looking down to see his complete stature. The more she looked, the more he seemed strange to her. At one point he appeared to her as if his eyes were abnormally too deep into their sockets. The more she talked to him, the higher her voice echoed anger, disappointment, and frustration.

When he asked his mother to leave and let him handle things in the manner he scripted, his voice was equally high; perhaps too high that the female officer who was watching and recording them went in, ended the meeting, and ordered Simeon back to his cell while his mother wiped her tears. Sephinia stood in the room for some minutes, gazing out the window. When she finally got herself together, she leaned and picked up her bag and slowly exited the room.

For many times they have observed and recorded Simeon in his cell. The decision to do so was approved at the highest level of the authority in an attempt to gather the details about him. When his mother requested to see him, it provided them a tangible opportunity to hear him in a conversation with someone to whom he could hold nothing back, or at least, reveal more. The recording of his meeting with his mother reinforced their conviction that he was responsible for the deaths of which he was accused. The clique that was looking for an opportunity to "terminate" his life has been shopping for the "perfect circumstance" to bring their objective to fruition.

The basement of this police unit hosts a large conference room where "sensitive" issues were discussed and "confidential" meetings held. This day, as several top officers and their leadership gather to watch the recordings of Simeon and evaluate their course of action, the conference room was adequately prepared with optimum audio and visual gadgets. As everyone settled comfortably in their various seats, the temperature was just perfect, and everything seemed orderly.

"We have been keeping tabs on Simeon's activities following the crimes for which he has been accused. We have some audio and video recordings, including the one done when his mother visited him recently. You are going to see some of those recordings, including the most recent one where he made it clear that some have fallen and that many more may follow. In the same recording, he bragged to his mother that he was the one in control and could handle the situation. Ladies and gentlemen," the female officer announced as she headed to a seat at the right front corner, "Simeon Rhenoake."

Everyone in the room remained attentive and focused on the large screen in front of them. However, the picture that came up was not what they had anticipated. Instead of the picture of Simeon, when the female officer pointed the remote control and pushed the play button, the lights in the room flickered on and off, then came a very strong, bright flash on the screen. It was so bright that everyone in the room instinctively looked away.

The whole room was brightly lit up as if it was an energy force of some sort, then it slowly dimmed to a yellowish figure, exactly the character of Simeon's tattoo, a figure they resolved to call Zeus. As if reacting to the people in the room, it turned to face them, and then it blinked. And just when they wondered if a wrong video was mistakenly put on, Zeus jumped out of the screen onto the floor. The few lights that were on went off as he landed very loudly on the floor in a very bright flash, the door of the conference room swung open, and footsteps were heard leaving the room. Everyone was in shock; they noticed when Zeus leaped out of the screen and the flash that landed, but no one saw anything else.

As they heard the footsteps exit the room, the door slammed shut as if there was a dead force that pushed it from behind. The temperature in the room immediately started climbing. As everyone started to build up some sweat, they rushed toward the door, yearning for some air, but the door would not open no matter how much force they applied.

As there was no option left, one of the men in the room took off his neck tie, grabbed the axe right next to the fire extinguisher and headed for the door. He was determined to break it down even if in pieces. He put all his energy behind the axe, determined to punch a hole through. But when the axe was about to make contact with the door, it swung ajar, and the axe sank into the face of the man that was on the other side coming inside the room. The security guard was coming to investigate the source of the noise they heard when the door slammed so hard against the frame. His death was instantaneous. He fell on his back with the axe remaining lodged in his face with blood and brain matter spilling out of him.

When the news of the event circulated, the group of five officers that met at Sheehan's funeral contacted each other and agreed to meet for a discussion at night after work. The chosen venue was a busy hotel parking lot, and appearance was to be in plain clothes.

At the meeting, the group reached a consensus to "waste" Simeon and sought to do so in the "most efficient" manner. They discussed various scenaria and concluded it needed to be carried out soon no matter the method. After trading methods and scenaria, they were unanimous on staging a scene where the conclusion would be that Simeon committed suicide. They ruled out any involvement with a gun. They concluded it would bring the type of attention, investigation, and scrutiny that they do not need.

By the time the meeting ended, their consensus was that "death by hanging" would be "his way out." In setting the stage, someone would have to go into his cell to execute the plan. It centered on having a plumber leave a towel long enough to hang someone inside his cell during the current maintenance call. The towel will be provided to the plumber who must be instructed to leave it there in the cell. The plan was to "silence" the plumber afterward. "Accidents do happen," one of the men added during the discussion.

"Do me a favor. Could you leave this towel in number 137 when you're in there," the officer pleaded as he buzzed the plumber through the security door.

"Number 137? Sure," he replied and accepted a long, narrow towel that was not particularly ideal for showers.

When the plumber entered Simeon's cell, he did not see him. He went about his inspection and made the necessary repairs he needed to make. When he completed all he needed to do, he exited the cell, leaving behind the pink towel just as he was instructed.

"Did you leave the towel for him in the cell?" the officer asked the plumber, eager to hear his wish confirmed.

"Yes sir," he replied.

The officer nodded firmly.

"Thank you, sir."

The officer proceeded to sit down, leaned back, and put a piece of chewing gum in his mouth as he rested his feet on the trash can he positioned under a desk. As officer Neiman relaxed in his seat, having been assured that the towel he supplied to the plumber had been placed as he requested, he suddenly felt there was some cold breeze around him. As he wondered about the sudden change in temperature, it continued to get increasingly colder to the point that he noticed some steam was coming from his breath. Before he could get up to see if it was just his immediate surrounding or a wider change in weather, he felt the chill drift past him as if it went toward the exit and left the building. He came out of the security booth anyway, wandered around, and went back to his seat. He reached for his cell phone and dispatched a text message: "The order has been delivered," and laid down the phone on his desk.

Mr. Neiman had barely taken his hand off the cell phone he just placed on his desk when the phone in his booth rang. As he reached for it, his cell phone also started ringing. And as he moved to attend to both phones, an officer came running toward him asking, "What's going on? I just heard on the radio—"

He put both phones on, one to each ear, only to hear his wife on the cell phone say, "I'm at home. You need to get here now," and hung up. Her voice was with panic.

On the other phone, a calm and respectful voice asked, "Mr. Neiman?"

"Yes, this is he," he answered.

"Sir, I'm at your residence. I think you need to be here, there's been a—"

He let go of the phone, reached into one of the drawers on his desk, took a loaded 9mm handgun, and stuffed it into his pocket. "Take over, Dan," he told the officer standing by the side and dashed toward the exit.

When Mr. Neiman arrived at his residence, he came into a scene that either had a major disaster written all over it or one that evidenced an assembly of the necessary tools and human capital used to salvage one. Fire trucks and ambulances were present, but the sight of two vans from the office of the coroner almost gave him a serious cardiac abnormality.

On his way from the station, he tried but was unable to find out what exactly was going on at his house. Now, however, he no longer needed anyone to tell him it was something bad when his vehicle was guided through the cordoned-off street and escorted right into his house.

Inside the house, he was immediately joined by a psychologist who started saying, "I know how difficult it must be, but the first thing is not to blame yourself because no one has all the answers why things like this happen."

Mr. Neiman could not hold his sanity any longer, "For God's sake, could someone tell me what the hell happened?"

"It's your son. He committed suicide, sir. He hung himself," the psychologist told him while her hands rested on his shoulder.

He was led into the room. "Here is where he was found. Some men from your office have the pink towel he used. It is in their custody as routine demands. I'm sure you understand."

"A towel? He used a pink towel? Where did he get the pink towel? It doesn't make any sense. It makes no sense at all." He continued talking to himself as he paced the floor, his head tilted downward as if he was searching the floor for some answers.

"What the hell happened?" one of the men that received Mr. Neiman's text asked. He and Mr. Neiman, along with three others had planned to "take care of" Simeon, whom they agreed was a problem, and reached a consensus to "terminate" his existence by hanging him in his cell in a manner that would seem as if he took his own life.

The more he paced the floor of his house, the more questions he was bothered with and so he resolved to head to the station for some answers. He was overwhelmed by eagerness to know more about how a towel that was supposed to be in Simeon's cell became the material with which his son killed himself, as he was just made aware. He excused himself and rushed out and into his car with his friend before others at his heels could catch up to him.

"I was told he hung himself with a pink towel. I have to see that towel. I have to see what towel it is before I go crazy. Could you come with me to forensics, please? Help me convince them I only need to see it. I don't even need to touch it but would like to do so with gloves if I could," he pleaded with the person that was in charge of the morgue.

"Where did he get this?" Mr. Neiman asked the lab technician holding the towel spread out between the two of them. "I'm sorry.

I'm really not thinking straight." He quickly realized he was asking the wrong person. They left the unit.

"It was the same towel I gave the plumber to leave in his cell. I did not see him with it when he came out, and he confirmed he left it in the cell. How that got to my house is what I'd like to find out. I intend to go into that cell to find out."

"You know what? Not right now," his colleague suggested. "Let me at least secure a sound suppressor before we pay him a visit. We cannot rule anything out."

"The sooner you do so, the better off we are. Things have begun to take an ugly shape, and I don't like it."

"I'll see what I can do."

Simeon was in his cell bed when Mr. Neiman and his friend entered the cell. His face was turned toward the wall with his back toward them. They could not tell if he was sleeping. As far as they observed, he neither moved nor made a sound. The noises they made to wake him were futile as he remained still. They initiated various moves to induce a reaction from him, or create a confrontational environment; however, he remained motionless even as one of them called his name out loud.

Mr. Neiman took his partner's baton; he wanted to strike it against a part of the bed to wake him. But as the baton was about to make contact with the bed, a wall of water barrier appeared between the baton and Simeon. They were startled as they both noticed what transpired. His instinctive reaction was to pull his hand, and as he did so, the object disappeared.

After a minute or so, Mr. Neiman tried to poke Simeon with the baton, and again the water shield became visible. Then he tried again, this time to hit him with the baton, hoping for a reaction of some sort from the shield; but before it could hit Simeon, they both saw Zeus stretch his hand and reach the baton and push hard against it that it hit Mr. Neiman and tore his upper lip.

Before the baton could hit the floor, Mr. Neiman had already reached for his gun and kept firing away, but Zeus blocked each shot using his hands, body, and horns as he stood fully upright. Simeon was no longer in the bed, and no one saw him get up or leave. He has either assumed Zeus, or Zeus has taken his body to function.

When no more bullets came out of Mr. Neiman's gun, he threw the gun toward Zeus just before what seemed like an iron hand reached out to his upper jaw while the other hand pulled his lower jaw and separated both in a split second. His lower jaw was only held hanging on some bare bloody strings of skin while blood filled his mouth. Mr. Neiman's partner did not wait to see the end of what they initiated; he had left Simeon's cell the minute he saw Zeus reach for his partner.

By the time medics got to Simeon's cell, they picked up the lifeless body of Mr. Neiman after they bandaged his torn jaw to his head. There was no sign of Simeon in the cell or anywhere around, and no one showed any interest about his whereabouts. The authority holding him would later decide on what next to do.

Since every attempt to silence Simeon Rhenoake has so far not only failed but backfired, the authority decided to set him free in an official manner. A certain group had discussed simply keeping his cell unlocked and somewhat unattended to see if he would simply leave. However, they later decided that a formal release would be more logical as they wanted him to have the impression that he was indeed free.

They contacted his mother and had her present as they announced, in a news conference, that charges would not be filed against him for lack of actionable evidence. The announcer turned to his mother and said, "Simeon is being released to his mother, and he is free to go about his life. We are removing the key and the lock from his cell door, and so he is hereby declared a free man and able to go about his business from this very moment."

Simeon met up with his mother right where she parked her vehicle only to tell her he was going back to his apartment. "Would you please stop worrying about me? I am an adult and can take care of myself," he promised his mother and started walking away as his mother watched him until he melted into the traffic.

That very evening, all the local news outlets described Simeon as demonically possessed. They cited that some reliable sources have intimated that he was capable of transforming into a beast equipped with destructive horns. Some termed him "the bullet proof man" who could catch speeding bullets with his bare hands. He has pretty much been baptized a monster despite the lack of evidence of any wrong doing that was pronounced by the same authority that cleared him of any crime.

At her house, Sephinia was also watching the evening news. She could hardly believe the manner they described her son and the titles imposed on him. Nevertheless, she continued watching since every channel had the story; but when one station attributed over ten deaths to Simeon, she could no longer hold it. With her head buried into both palms, she broke into tears.

Later when she wiped her eyes, she resolved to contact her former husband to let him know that their son needs help. She decided she would start with talking Simeon into a visit with a psychiatrist, and then changed her mind after arguing with herself that he has not shown any detectable sign of mental abnormality. She settled to see what she could do to take him to a psychologist first.

As the psychologist sat in front of Sephinia and her son, she explained to the doctor that her son had recently been showing an intense level of anger, a high degree of sadness, and mean demeanor. With tears in her eyes, she asked the doctor for help.

When he asked Simeon the cause and source of his episodes, he did not admit to any abnormality. "I do not think that anyone admires an abuse no matter what form, and I am yet to meet anyone that rejoices for being victimized, ridiculed, taken advantage of, and abused. I just happen to be no different than many people, and so whenever such a situation presents itself, I stand up against it," he concluded.

He went on to engage in more exchanges with the psychologist, who didn't particularly see eye to eye with him on any subject. However, they both ended on a civil note.

"May I have a word with you, ma'am?" the psychologist requested of Sephinia, who abruptly got up and followed him to a different room. He shut the door behind them.

"Listen," he began as he looked her dead in the face, "I can tell you with absolute certainty that in my professional opinion, your son did not exhibit anything that will indicate the existence of the least psychological abnormality. If the issue was of a medical nature, that would be different, but certainly not a psychological, or psychiatric problem for that matter.

"Here is what I will suggest for your own peace of mind. Get a confirmation that he is in perfect medical shape. Have them do some blood work, MRI, whatever scan so that you are sure. For your own sanity, so to speak. It does not do me any good wasting your time or imposing some unnecessary costs on you, and it does not help you either."

Sephinia remained silent, just kept staring at the doctor for a few minutes. Then she promised the doctor that she would do exactly what he advised. "I will take your advice, at least for my own peace of mind if for nothing else. Could you help me convince him to go that extra mile if that's what it would take to leave him alone as he would like?" she requested of the psychologist.

"I will see what I can do," he replied.

When Simeon and his mother arrived at Melyena Inland Diagnostics, he headed to a water fountain as he told his mother that he was thirsty and needed to get some water. She stood there in the large hall, waiting for him, watching him drink an amount of water she thought was impossible for one person at one time. "You couldn't possibly be that thirsty. That is just not possible. I just watched you drink no less than a gallon of water. Where did all that go? I think there is something truly wrong for anyone to drink that much water all at once. That was enough to drown your lungs. Have you always had that much water at a time? Ever drank that much before, Simeon?"

"Mom, I was just thirsty, and I had the amount of water that I needed to quench my thirst. That's all."

"Well, let's go in and see these people. Make sure you let them know how much you drink whenever you're thirsty because I don't think it's normal. I have never seen anyone, anyone at all, drink that much water at one time. Some people don't even drink that much in days."

When he was called, the receptionist advised him, "You are going to have a few tests done today. We need to get your MRI done first. When you finish, you need to come here again and wait to be called for your next test. You'll go into that room for your blood sample to be drawn, and they'll give you further instructions about collecting your urine sample and so on. Do you have any question?"

"No, I'm good."

"Once you pass that door, there'll be someone to take you from there." Pointing to a door at the end of a short hallway, the receptionist motioned him away.

Simeon took off his shorts and changed into the gown given to him, listened to the instructions given, got onto the machine slide, and then rolled into the chamber for a full body scan. Inside the scanning chamber, he closed his eyes and went into a trance. It was as if he was journeying through space at quantum speed with stars, large and small, dim and bright, zooming by until he reached a tranquil state.

In his trance, he could see he was still at a very high speed and the surrounding was all sky blue. He thought it was very peaceful and refreshingly tranquil. He noticed he was steadily approaching what seemed like a mirage, changing reflections as he got closer. But as he reached right in front of the mirage, every motion stopped, and a figure stepped out of what was the mirage—or the mirage transformed into a male-like figure.

A tall, slim figure with gray hair and long gray beard with no eyes in the deep sockets "looked" in Simeon's direction when he came to a stop. He watched the "old man" tilt his head as if he were looking to see something that was behind him. But before Simeon could find out what the old man was looking at, another figure, short and stubby, emerged from behind him and stood beside the old man. When the figure turned to face Simeon, he noticed it was the exact character that he tattooed on his leg standing right in front of him. It was Zeus.

The old man raised his hand, and a feather appeared. He put the feather to the front of Simeon's left elbow. Simeon tried to step back as his hand reached toward him, but he could not. He realized he was under paralysis and could not move any part of his body, although he was aware of the things around him. He felt the hard end of the feather pierce into his elbow. He could not resist it piercing through his skin no matter how hard he tried.

As the old man retracted his hand, Simeon saw a drop of blood on the feather. It was perfectly round, like a ball bearing. The old man raised his left hand, and an ancient mini pot appeared. It looked perfectly smooth. He thought it must have been sculpted from clay.

Zeus remained motionless; he just remained standing. The old man tilted the feather toward the pot's opening, and the blood dropped inside. Then he stretched his left hand a little to the left, and as he did, a clear stream of liquid poured into the pot. It was a small pot, but the water that poured in seemed like it could have filled up the cup some thirty times over. When it finally stopped, the old man stirred the cup with the feather. The feather disappeared instantly when he held the pot with both hands in front of his chest, and a lid slowly descended onto the pot and sealed it shut.

The pot gave out a reddish glow while some yellowish steam slowly poured out from all around it. Slowly, it floated away from the old man's grasp and rested in the front between him and Zeus, spinning as it remained there. The lid opened and let out a more intense cloud of steam. A headless falcon and vulture emerged from the pot, followed by a woodpecker with its head and beak.

As the pot spun in one direction, the falcon and vulture circled in the other direction. As if it was standing guard, the woodpecker remained stationery until everything else came to a stop. Then it walked to the pot and dipped its beak; and as it raised its head, the beak was transparent that the blood in its mouth was visible. The woodpecker walked over to Zeus, dipped its beak and emptied the blood into him. As the woodpecker pulled its beak off him, Zeus blinked three times, then walked over to Simeon's foot and melted into him. Simeon felt a sudden pressure but could not move; he only stared as the birds and the old man slowly turned into what once again seemed like a mirage.

"Did you fall asleep, sir?" the MRI technician asked Simeon.

"What happened?" Simeon asked in reply as he quickly examined his left arm and noticed his elbow had been bandaged. "What is this?"

"That's where I gave you the contrast. Do you not remember I said you would have contrast after the initial scan? It was injected in that arm."

"I'm sorry. I fell asleep in there."

"Hey, if you could sleep through all that noise, that's even better for you. We are done here. You are free to go. Here is the key to the locker where you put your clothes. Just leave the gown in the basket in the room and walk on out to the hall."

"Thank you, sir," Simeon responded and left the room.

"Okay, your next stop is there," the receptionist informed him, pointing to an adjacent door. "That is where you need to be for your next procedure."

Simeon blinked again and again. With each successive blink, he noticed that his eyesight was becoming sharper and sharper. By the time he opened the door and seated in front of the young lady holding a small tray with syringe and vials in it, his eyesight had become so sharp that he could see the internal organs of the person in front of him. He felt he was looking or seeing through an X-ray machine. He looked straight down to the floor, kept his eyes closed for a minute or so, looked at her again, and was still able to see her internal organs. He looked straight at her face and their eyes met.

"Are you all right?" she asked.

"Oh, yes, of course. I'm fine."

"I guess it's going to be your right hand."

"Yes, that will be just fine."

Simeon felt anxious. He seemed preoccupied, perhaps confused as his mind was busy wondering what was going to happen next; and no matter how calm he attempted to portray, his wandering eyes betrayed his calm attitude. He managed to sit through the rest of his tests with his mind preoccupied with questions for which he could not get to an answer.

When he and his mother returned to find out the outcome of his tests, they were both told that the MRI result did not reveal any abnormality. They were told that the test failed to show anything wrong with him and, hence, ruled that everything looked all right as far as the images were concerned.

The outcome of the blood test was equally ruled as being normal except for one inconsistency that was present in the blood. The diagnostic pathologist that examined the blood explained that there was just one thing in the blood they were not able to define, adding they could not identify whether it was a string of bacteria or not. In fact, they were not quite sure if it was a living thing at all but certainly not something that one would expect in the bloodstream. She said it was impossible to separate the thing from the blood around it except by cutting it out, that it bonded itself to the blood and must be excised to separate it.

She went on to explain that there was an attempt to stimulate it with electricity to preempt a reaction, but no reaction occurred. "We thought it might be bacteria or virus, but all the tests so far conducted showed it lacked the characteristics of any living thing. It is just there. The next thing we need to do is to examine it under an electron microscope. That will be more definitive. We have managed to schedule one for next week. We will let you know of the outcome," she concluded.

She got up to leave the room but sat down again. "May I ask why you wanted his blood examined in the first place? Was he exhibiting any symptoms? Was there anything out of the ordinary? I mean, is he sick?"

"It's just that he has not been himself lately. He sleeps too much, his thirst for water is in the range I would consider abnormal, and if recent news meant anything, he is guilty of having powers that are not humanly possible. Need I say more?"

"I see. Well, his brain scan seems normal, or else I would have raised an alarm. Why don't we do this? Let's just wait till we have put the specimen in his blood through the electron microscope and analyzed the outcome. And if nothing stands out, then I will recommend something else to you. I will contact you as soon as I get some results. Let's take it one step at a time. I wouldn't panic if I were you."

When Simeon and his mother left that day, he told his mother he was fine and did not plan to return to the facility as long as he did not fall ill. He had accepted all the changes in him, the ones that were obvious to him, and delighted in his sharpened reflexes, which, to himself at least, he recognized to be out of the ordinary.

When Simeon went to bed that night, he found himself unable to fall asleep. He remained in his bed awake, despite how tired and worn down he felt. As his eyes wandered around in his bedroom, he saw vultures coming and leaving. They repeatedly flew in, landed in the room, and then left in the opposite direction.

He remained motionless while the episode repeated itself. He felt frozen and unable to move any part of his body for the duration the vultures made their visits. When he was finally able to move his feet, the one that was about to enter the room turned around and changed course rather than fly into the room. He sat on the edge of his bed, trying to overcome the weakness that temporarily took control of his motor functions. It was not clear to him if what he just experienced was an actuality or whether it was another episode of weird dreams. He managed to get to his feet for some water. Nearly a gallon of water afterward, he returned to bed and fell asleep.

When he transitioned into a deep state of sleep, he found himself walking a narrow winding path. It was wet and lightly foggy. As he turned a corner, he came to a stop when he noticed that what he thought was a huge pile of dirt was indeed a graveyard of many vultures. As he stood there looking closely, it seemed to him like the place where vultures came to die.

Even as he looked, he noticed that more and more of the birds fall straight out of the sky onto the pile. He thought of the ones that passed through his bedroom. In his mind, it was a dream, but then he questioned how it could be a dream when he was not asleep as it all unfolded. *Am I now able to dream even when I'm awake?* he thought. Then again, he concluded it must be a dream because the door and windows of the room were not only shut, but securely locked.

As he watched other birds join the pile of dead ones, he heard a loud voice coming across. It was as if it traveled through the foggy chill to the sole destination, which happens to be right where he stood. He could not make out the words, but the waves kept carrying the voice toward him. He continued, heading in the direction of the voice, and the farther he trekked, the louder the voice grew, punctuated only by intermittent sounds of a bell.

With each step he advanced, it seemed the voice was equally moving farther away from his position until he slowed down ahead of a dense fog. More cautious than usual as the fog grew even more dense, he noticed the voice sounded quite far away, and the bell still tolled. When he made it beyond the fog, at a distance was a tall black bearded man dressed in a red robe that stretched almost to the ground.

As he closed in, he noticed the robe was accented with a yellow belt woven of cloth around his waist with the two-piece extension dangling down past his left knee. Even at his close proximity, Simeon was still unable to understand what he was saying; he could only hear him and the sound of the bell in his right hand. What he could not understand was that no matter how hard he tried to get closer to the man, the distance between them remained the same even as he was sure the man was not moving. He was standing on a spot and looking at a direction that was, to Simeon, foggier than the rest of the surroundings. He occasionally pointed toward the area of the dense fog with his left hand.

As Simeon looked at the area with the dense fog, he noticed that although it was raining all around there, he could not see the rain descend on the ground. It looked cold and desolate, like a place under a curse. It had a cold, stale smell, like a place that could not nurture life. From what he could make of the grass below the fog, they did not look as if they had much life in them.

He stopped walking. He felt reluctant to look behind him, fearing there might be something he would not want to see. He kept looking at the man from the distance. As he looked at him, he thought of the biblical John the Baptist.

From behind him came a sound piercing through the foggy chill. It sounded like a cry from a falcon, but he declined to look back. Right next to him at his left, a big drop of blood splattered as it hit the ground. A headless falcon flew past him toward the man he now called "the prophet" with a trail of blood as it disappeared farther into the fog. When he stopped looking at the bird and looked down, he found himself standing where the prophet was, but the prophet was no longer there, although his voice and the sound of his bell sounded as if they were both standing next to each other. The words from the prophet were now distinctively discernible to him as he stood there with eyes fixed at what was only a dense fog earlier.

A vast graveyard stretched as far as his eyes could see. There was a gray cloud hanging over the vast area and an eerie stillness that conveyed death in every way. Everything seemed dead and still that not even the grass swayed in any direction. There was this certain absence of wind.

As the prophet's message continued on, he listened attentively with enthusiasm. He was consumed with contentment about the extent to which the voice quite soothed the moment and the desolate surrounding. The voice continued,

> *"This field of the dead,*
> *Morrow I set my gaze at the graveyard of old*
> *Where the dead remains forever silent*
> *And objects decay through time that bore them.*
> *For time has no beginning, and every beginning*
> *Only marked by time.*
> *Every event predestined and realization*
> *Merely a spot of light cast by time.*
> *Time is God, and God is time,*
> *No beginning and never shall end."*

Simeon felt as if he was in transition to what he could not tell. The prophet's message was not just audible to him, but the reception went beyond his hearing. He felt that there was a cold wind that descended from the above to his head and down the rest of his body to the ground he stood on. He felt transformed. Although the things around him were still not clearly distinctive, he noticed that there was more clarity in the things he was surrounded with.

> *"Here lies a tomb of fancy and decor.*
> *This one once the source of misery for many*

*Now reduced to mere waste where worms feast.
How lies that the evil bequeaths to them
That reason not and defile the innocent.
For he is not yet content with the loot,
And no boundary for him will stand unviolated,
Lest his curse be abridged and His words in doubt.
Morrow his feet will stand on a new land, and
A virgin will stand defiled."*

Then the voice started to faint; and as it did, darkness descended over the horizon. Simeon decided it was time to leave; and as he turned around, there was a headless falcon with fresh blood inside a coffin right beside him. He was sure it was not there earlier when he came; and as he tried to get himself together, the falcon got out of the coffin and headed directly toward the graveyard where it disappeared.

He was startled to the extent that he instinctively jumped back; and as he did, he heard a faint sound of someone calling his name. "Simeon, Simeon, wake up."

He slowly opened his eyes and noticed that he was surrounded by people with the only familiar face being that of his mother. "You had me going crazy, Simeon. It's been five days since you were brought here at the hospital."

He looked up at his mother whose tears were running down her cheeks.

"Five days with no one able to find what was wrong or what to do. Five days," she sobbed as she looked down at her son lying on the bed. "They've had to feed you with tubes, son. There was not a test in the world they did not perform on you, and not a single soul could find anything wrong. You put a lot of people in suspense, and I'm not sure yet if I'm not insane."

What Simeon remembered was that he went to sleep in his own bed. As far as he was concerned, it did not seem he slept for too long until he was made aware that he not only overslept but was in a comatose for nearly a week. It would take a lot of convincing to get him to accept that he had slept for five days. He was cognizant of what occurred in his sleep, and even that seemed normal.

He could not wholly accept to himself that he had woken up after a long dream that lasted for five days. He just lay there looking at those around him from one to the other, but his eyes rested more on one of the medical personnel. And as they kept asking how he felt, he calmly responded, "I'm fine. I'm quite all right. I would appreciate it if these gadgets could be undone and taken off me, please," making a gesture to the wires and tubes attached to his body.

"Excuse me, sir," he motioned to the one person he'd had his eyes on.

"Could I have some privacy while he takes these things off me, please?"

He was calm and polite as he leaned toward the man and asked, "Everything okay?"

The man responded in the affirmative, adding, "It would be okay if you tell us that you are. We believe you since we have not been able to find any abnormality."

"I meant, is everything all right with you?"

"I'm quite well, sir."

"No, I really mean it. Are you all right? You don't look so well, and I mean that sincerely?"

"We're here to take care of you as we've been doing for the past four days or so, sir," the response was with anger as he reminded Simeon that he was the patient and not the other way around. "Our job is to diagnose and treat you as long as you remain admitted here as a patient."

"I did not mean to take anything away from you, sir, but please do get your gallbladder checked out," Simeon responded.

"Excuse me?"

"The sooner you do so, the better."

"I'll get someone to detach the connectors and move the monitor for you." The man left angrily, his name unknown to Simeon.

As he insisted he was ready to walk out of the hospital if they declined to discharge him, they buckled and accommodated his demand; he was effectively discharged. Just before he left the hospital, his mother received a phone call advising her to come to Dr. Günther's office on Wednesday for the result of the electron microscope examination. They scheduled the time for the visit, and they both left the hospital.

"Sephinia, I'm sorry that the only progress I have to report is one that I myself do not understand," Dr. Günther told Sephinia as they sat opposite each other.

"I don't understand."

"I must say it's quite strange. Each time we tried to analyze the sample using the electron scope, the object in the blood sample was not visible. It did not matter what or how we manipulate the sample. It's particularly not visible on the scope. It is not detectable when the equipment that is best suited to shade a light on what it is was turned on.

"What is even more interesting is that when we varied the measurement ranges to defeat the invisibility, things went off course. The lights in the room flickered, the cooling system for the microscope stopped working, and three of the shutters in the windows broke apart and fell on the floor, while the doors to the main facility entrance came off their welded hinges, shattering all the glasses. It is absurd. The equipment overheated for no apparent reason.

"It's even utterly senseless that I am relating the two to each other. I hope the information does not leave this room, for sanity's sake."

"I'm sorry, but I still don't understand," Sephinia interjected.

"Well, that was our realization, that we were dealing with something that extended beyond modern technology and normal medical practice."

Sephinia just sat motionless, her eyes rested at Dr. Günther, unable to wrap her head around what she was being told and so could not come up with a word to express what was going through her head. It was just five days ago that she was called to come for the outcome of the exam. As she sat there listening to her, that outcome was nothing that made any sense to her.

"Let me try to explain to you what I am getting at," the doctor continued. "You know how you walk into a doctor's office sometimes and there's a Bible among the other reading materials? That is because we have come to accept that there are things we just cannot explain.

Things that we just do not know or understand. And so the only prescription we can truly give is the opportunity to explore other areas."

Then she got up from her seat. "If it's all right with you, I'd like to have someone contact you. She's a person knowledgeable about nonconventional treatments, the type of which I think we're dealing with here. If you want to think about it first, that'll be understandable, but it must not be next week. We lost one of our staff last week, and his funeral has been set for next week, so I'm fully committed all next week."

"Funny that doctors themselves are not immune to death." Sephinia responded.

"You know," Dr. Günther said, "there is a common saying among the Biafran Jews that when translated to English means 'a doctor found the cure for one disease, but another disease killed the doctor.' They use the phrase to tell us that no one is immune to death, that no matter what, everyone eventually gets to die. The man that died, however, was one of our associates, not a doctor."

"So he died of an unknown, incurable disease?"

"No. Not quite," she quipped. "His gallbladder ruptured. It was so bad that much of his internal organs were fatally poisoned by the time help got to him."

"Oh my, bless his soul."

When Ralph Ingram discussed what he termed an encounter with Simeon, he could not conceal his disdain for him to his coworker, Rose Blanchard. Moreover, even as she stood and watched Mr. Whitaker narrate the episode in confirmation, she struggled to make sense out of the narratives. "Did you tell him you were having a problem with your gallbladder or was he just a psychic wannabe?" she asked.

For all it was worth, they both traded jokes about Simeon, ranging from his mental state to labeling him a complete "jackass." It was not until she heard about Ralph's death that she took an alternate route, and she did not keep things to herself.

It was not long after the death of Ralph Ingram that Rose Blanchard went public with what she discussed with him about Simeon. She was out for castigation, saying to everyone that paid attention that

Simeon was something from Satan itself. She went around town calling for his public execution, saying he would be a suitable candidate for stoning or any form of public execution. She did not have to carol around for too long before she gathered sizable supporters, among whom "Simeon Rhenoake" had not only become a familiar name but an incredibly notorious one. They joined forces with Ms. Blanchard to demand that something be done about Simeon.

Things got off hand when Ms. Blanchard and her faithful membership surrounded Ms. Rhenoake's residence and demanded she bring out her son for "crucifixion," wielding weapons that range from machetes, pickaxes, knives, and pistols. They ignored the mother's plea to leave her premises, that Simeon was not in her house.

For whatever reason, law enforcement did not immediately come to her aid despite repeated calls. It was not until their ear-piercing siren was heard that the crowd disappeared, having vowed to come back even more determined to take matters into their own hands, adding that her son's menace had been allowed to go on for too long.

They had all spirited away when it became obvious to Sephinia that the siren was not from a vehicle destined for her residence. She went into her house and headed to pour herself a sizable amount of liquor and gulped it down. She leaned down, stared into the kitchen sink for a while, and then headed to the phone to call her son.

"If I hadn't heard it from Dr. Günther myself, I would have believed the mob that besieged my house that you killed that man we met at the hospital," she relayed to her son. "I was just hounded by a mob that was asking for your head, saying you killed Mr. Ingram. I am baffled. I just do not understand it—"

"Are they still there, mom?" he interrupted as his mother kept talking. "If they are still there, I want to come and put them in their places. The more they are, the better so that this city can have its first mass funeral. The time has gone when I was interested in babysitting any fool that came around and spoon-fed the idiots. I see they have all left, but that does not get them off the hook, not while I am still alive. Tomorrow, one by one their clouds will begin to close in. I see their footprints, and therein lay their demise. Let this city prepare to bury its dead. Let them be put on notice."

Simeon had gone from the passive person he once was to a bold, assertive person that has recognized his endowment of certain powers, good or bad, and very poised to explore them. At the beginning, his powers were in control of him; events occurred beyond his will and actions driven by powers he neither understood nor commanded. Wherever he found himself were merely destinations he was driven to by the powers that superseded his will. None of his actions were preplanned by him. He was merely driven, just as a passenger in a vehicle for which the destination he neither determined nor knew.

Gradually, he gained more powers and at a point graduated to being in command of those powers. But even when he was assertive, it was still unclear to him what propelled him to make bold pronouncements. Even after the exchange with his mother, he would only remember that he started asking if those that confronted her had left. Everything else that came off his mouth was something he neither planned nor wanted to say, and he was not aware if he could do anything or not.

However, his words were so convincing that his mother gripped herself when she heard him call for the city to prepare for mass funerals. The words took her by surprise and sent chills right down her spine. She wondered whether she really knew her son or if something had gone terribly wrong. Millions of thoughts raced through her mind in a very short time. She could not help but ask him what he meant; however, no matter how hard she pressed, not one answer to her many questions ever came.

It was 1:20 in the morning when the city's police department received the first call through its emergency line. The caller reported she had just made it home after a night out only to see the decapitated body of her roommate. She said it must have been some wild animal because the apartment's entrance door was wide open when she arrived. But the ambulance had barely cleared a quarter mile before it was instructed to a different location, one that was closer than the one for which the ambulance was dispatched.

It was not long before it became apparent that something sinister had started. The calls kept coming, each report resembling the one earlier of gory descriptions, mutilations, butchering, scattered body parts. Each report described things that resemble scenes out of horror movies. The sirens touched nearly every street that many residents came out of their homes and apartments to stand on the outside, fearing that remaining inside might engender something ominous.

The responders were reporting of dissected bodies, missing internal organs, severed lungs, and everything else that is indeed incomprehensible as if it were only some weird fiction and not real. Within a span of three hours and seventeen minutes, the city had registered seventeen such calls. They termed it "bloody dawn."

It did not take long for the news to circulate as the sun forced a change on the surface below it. It swirled and flew like wildfire all over the city and beyond. The law enforcement was too busy and overwhelmed that there were not enough men left to embark on the detective work.

As the news of the event became common knowledge, even those at work were calling families, friends, and loved ones. Some that have already made it to work decided it was more important to be at home with their loved ones or at places they deemed more reassuring than to remain at work. The streets were beyond chaotic, the traffic a clear indication of what it would be should a major disaster hit the city to the extent that what is regarded as the normal, civilized manner of behavior is quickly forgotten. It was a miracle that the only noticeable difficulty with the phone lines was frequent busy signals and long wait before connections were established.

The authorities already had a culprit in mind, and they did not lack the written pages to convince anyone that would otherwise not buy what they had for sale. They had, in their capacity, legal or not, attempted all manner of approaches, including extra judicial acts, but could not score a success. Even an outright assassination attempt backfired against those who sought to carry it out in order to assert justice as they saw it. They went the way of the outcome they intended for their victim. Even as others continued nursing some ideas, those ideas would only remain in their heads never to be actualized. That fear of the unknown would always haunt many minds, yet there would always be those so daring they would try repeatedly to change the outcome.

When Sephinia started answering her phone that early morning, she could hardly believe the insults that were being directed toward her, nor did she have any inkling what she could have done to deserve them. When she took one of those calls, she was advised to stop. "Lady, we got your message. You can now call in your dog," the caller said.

She responded without hesitation, "What dog are you talking about? I'm Sephinia."

"Your son, lady. Your son. You can stop the killing now."

As she sat there changing from one channel to the next, and every one of them stuck on the same news, she reached her phone and called her son. She made several more attempts, but no one answered. She dashed into a room, came out with a scarf over her head, dark shades over her eyes, and headed for her car.

As her car screeched to a stop at Simeon's place, she was opening his front door just about the same time her car door slammed shut. She saw her son sitting on his bed. He looked so tired and weak, so thin she could not believe how it was possible to have lost that much weight in such a short notice. His hair was very untidy; and when he looked up to her, his eyes were sunk deep inside their sockets and his whole countenance was expressionless.

On the floor were three empty containers that once held what amounted to three gallons of water. He turned his face back to the floor without a word as his mother stood there.

"Are you all right, Simeon? You look like a ghost. Have you not been eating?"

It did not matter what she said or asked; he did not respond. She shook his shoulder, tapped him on the arm. He did not utter a word. "Do you want something to eat? Should I bring you something to eat or drink?"

He offered no response.

"I am going to call 911. You do not look too well."

He would not respond. She reached over to the phone and dialed a call. But when she gave the address, she was informed that the emergency medical services would not go to that address. When she enquired as to why, she was advised that the city would not allow the vehicle or personnel dispatched to that address. When she demanded more, she was advised she could go to the city council and file a petition, and the call ended while she still had the earpiece to her ear.

She went to his closet and came out with some pants and a shirt. "Put these on, Simeon. I will drive you to the hospital myself." She rested the clothes on his right shoulder. "Do you want something to eat first? You now look like one of those Africans they show on TV, hungry and starved. Let me go and get you something to eat first while you freshen up and get dressed."

On her way to getting him something to eat, she decided she'll take a gamble despite it being early hours of the morning and made a call. "This is Sephinia. Is Dr. Günther in today? I need to see her. It's an emergency. I need to bring in my son. Please, I need to bring him in now."

"Ma'am, let me see if that will at all be possible. She just happened to be early this morning for some other things she needs completed before consulting with patients. Can I call you right back?"

"Yes, please. He's in a very bad shape right now. I need immediate intervention, please."

It was not long before her phone rang. "Ms. Rhenoake? This is Dr. Günther. Are you already on your way here"

"No, Dr. Günther. I want to get him something to eat, but we can be there in about forty-five minutes."

"And what exactly is wrong this time?"

"I went to see him this morning, and he was skinny to the bone. He looked like a ghost. You would not even recognize him now. He is not talking. He looks so frail. He needs immediate attention."

"But you are really not sure of any medical problem, are you?" Go ahead and bring him in, but I would like to talk to you when you come in."

"See you in a few minutes. Thank you, Dr. Günther."

When they arrived at Dr. Günther's office, they did not have to wait for long before Simeon was called in and his vitals taken. He was returned to the waiting area, and the outcome of his vitals was sent to the doctor.

When Sephinia returned from retrieving her phone from her car, Simeon had gone in to see the doctor. He came out not long since he went in for examination, and his mother was summoned by the doctor. "Nice to see you again, Ms. Rhenoake, if I may say so."

"Sephinia. Please call me Sephinia."

Dr. Günther started, "I have just seen Simeon. As far as I could tell, he looked all right to me. I did not see the emergency or the need for a medical attention that you expressed. He seemed pretty organized to me, and I was unable to make out the need for the type of critical condition that you expressed. Perhaps a slight increase in calorie intake would do, but I fail to see the need for emergency. In other words, he looked just fine to me."

"No, Dr. Günther, something is seriously wrong. I have never seen my son that skinny, nor have I ever seen his eyes so sunk in. I thought maybe he was hungry, but he did not even touch the food I brought him. Have you heard what they are saying about him? I cannot take it anymore. I don't have that much strength. I just can't." She went on and on as tears poured down her cheeks.

"I did not have time to hear everything that's been in the news. And I must confess, I don't think I ever will. We only have twenty-four hours in the day, and that's barely enough for the more important things I have to do. News, unfortunately, fails to make that priority list.

"Remember what I told you not long ago about other cures for other ailments or illnesses or conditions?"

"Yes."

"I think this may be the time to explore other avenues since there's really nothing in particular that we can definitively point our fingers to. Give me just a minute, please, Sephinia."

Dr. Günther summoned her nurse over the intercom. "Emily, would you bring Simeon in here and take his blood pressure and pulse again. Please take the reading from both of his arms. Thank you."

As he came into the doctor's office, Sephinia jumped up as she took a quick look at him, her mouth wide open. She looked at Dr. Günther, turned to his son, opened both of her arms—no word out of her mouth. Everyone stood still, looking at one another.

"Is something the matter?" Dr. Günther asked as she looked directly at Sephinia while waving Emily toward the thermometer hanging on the corner wall.

After making a few more gestures, some words finally came out. "What happened? Did you give him some magic shots or what? He did not look like this when we came in here."

She then turned to her son and asked, "Did you eat something or take something? Anything?"

"He looked just the same as I saw him a while ago, and I don't think there's anything known to man that could have transformed him as rapidly as you seem to express."

"Dr. Günther, could you please check with your staff, those that saw us when we came so that they can confirm to you what I'm saying. I am beginning to worry whether it's me that needs help. Am I going insane?"

"I'm going to give you a name and phone number that you can contact if you think that certain things are out of the ordinary. Remember our conversation a while back. Modern medicine does not have all the answers, and I don't think it ever will." She handed her a piece of paper. "I don't think you will need to see me again unless…" She extended her hand to Sephinia. "Good luck."

From the time they left Dr. Günther's office for Simeon's apartment, they did not exchange a word. She seemed quite preoccupied, although her son did not seem to care about a thing in the world. The atmosphere was that of utmost uncertainty. The only thing certain was that uncertainty abound.

When Sephinia finally approached her house, having dropped off her son, not particularly sure how she had managed to have made it thus far, she found a handful of young men and women run into a waiting van, and they took off just as she got closer. As she drove up her driveway, she found it littered with trash. Pieces of paper, broken bottles, and plastic bags stuffed with trash and leaves all around, and graffiti defaced the driveway.

Her rage was at its summit as she pushed in her front door and headed straight to the phone handset that was on her formal dining table and dialed 911. The response she received was neither comforting nor reassuring, but she waited for a dispatch.

When she had waited for what was then approaching two and a half hours since calling the police and no one in sight, she started feeling even more insecure. She called her son, with tears down her aging cheeks, she relayed what happened and the level of vulnerability she was feeling.

Simeon could not contain himself, and his anger was at such a high level that he could not disguise. "Mom, get out of that house right now. Do me a favor. Take your cell phone with you and drive to the GPX Mart. When you get there, park in one of the spaces to the left of the car wash. Shut the front door when you leave but leave it unlocked."

He hurriedly put on his shirt and stormed out of his apartment. When he made it to his mother's driveway, for whatever reason he collected all the trash that littered around and bagged them. He proceeded to collect samples of the graffiti, pulled up his shirt and proceeded to rub the ink all over his skin. He went on to use the water hose to clean what was left of the ink off the driveway.

When he finished, he went into the house and called his mother. "Mom, you can come home now. I have cleaned the driveway and picked up the trash. The city will not wake up with those that were responsible. They had all carried out their silly antics for their very last time. The sun will rise without their consciousness. You can come home now, Mom."

"Simeon, Simeon, you wait there. I'm on my way," Sephinia requested of him. However, he left the house the very second he hung up and headed to his apartment.

Sephinia was glad to see her driveway as clean as she had not seen it in a long time. She felt more than relieved that all the trash in the front lawn, the broken glasses, everything had all been cleaned up. She had anticipated seeing him there, but he was nowhere around. She wanted to call and thank him, but the minute she picked up the phone, she felt completely out of energy. Feeling too weak to even stand up, she let herself into the couch in her living room where she parted way with consciousness.

The character that Simeon tattooed on his leg has taken over his feature. Its face was exactly like Simeon's, and the only discernible difference was that anyone who knew him would agree he lost a few inches off his height and has grown horns. When the character that had become Simeon went from one place to the other, house to house serving what he called justice, everyone that knew him understood who he was but only wondered how he had become a shorter person than the Simeon they knew.

It surprised his mother that those they met as she walked behind her son did not seem to take notice of her. They only had the expression that revealed they knew Simeon but did not care about the person that was right on his heels.

As he walked into each house, she remained right in front of the entrance door from where she was able to see him walk straight into a room and out in a flash. She watched him put a palm leaf on each door, turn around, never to look back.

They went house to house from dawn, all afternoon, and into the sunset. It seemed as if darkness was rapidly approaching; and with each change, she saw Simeon quicken his steps, putting more distance between the two of them. From her position, she saw him turn around to face her; he stood there for a few seconds, and then turned into an alley just as a glowing short figure split from his side. For a second or so, they walked beside one another until the image disappeared into the alley.

Awakened by the loud thunder, she lay there feeling very tired and a bit shaky. She glanced around her as it thundered repeatedly, the loudness of it only accented by the forceful downpour. She simply remained in the leather couch wondering about the dream she just had. She thought about calling her son, but the thundering rain was loud enough, and the temperature was dropping fast.

She got up, went into her kitchen from where she heard a faint sound of a siren. It had been hours since she called the police and no longer interested in their intervention. She took a glass from the cabinet and went on to pour herself a drink, sank herself into a sofa, and turned on the television. The clock has passed eleven o'clock and ticking toward midnight.

The scene coming out of the television was as odd as the dream she had and just as weird. In all the local stations was breaking news, each channel alternating from one scene to another. At first, they showed a video of two dead turtles left in front of the police station. There were two dead turtles with a long palm leaf in the middle and a skunk at the base of the palm leaf. They said that no one knew how they got there, only that some people came outside when they could no longer bear the stench. When they did, they stumbled onto the scene.

When she changed the channel to save herself the disgust, she flipped unto a more goring scene. The city authorities were seen packing and hauling off body parts and organs from various locations. They went further to say that a palm leaf was left in the entrance of each residence from where they packed up human remains in body bags and some organs in igloo containers. The parts included some hearts that were still throbbing when the employees of the coroner's office reached the scene.

Sephinia was about to change the channel again when she heard her son's name mentioned. She kept it on the same channel as they went on to name him as the prime suspect. In fact, they announced he was the only one that had the mendacity to commit any crime of the magnitude. As she kept on watching in suspense, her gaze was framed and her mouth open, but she was unable to utter a word. Then, as if she just came out of a trance, she glanced around the room, walked over to where she left her keys, and paused for a few minutes. She just stared at the keys, then reached and grabbed them unusually firmly and got out the door.

It was raining very heavily when she pulled up in front of Simeon's apartment; it was raining quite heavily. The entire city was under a flood watch, and the advisory was to seek higher grounds. She braved it all and got out of her car. With the water level already past her ankles, she picked her way to the front of his door. It swung open effortlessly to reveal a scene that almost stopped her heart. On the floor was her son, his body wrapped with all manner of trash;

every piece of trash that was left at her house by the group that picketed her house, including the ink used to deface the concrete on her driveway, was salvaged and painted on his body. Simeon lay there motionless like a corpse.

When Sephinia dashed toward him, she found herself unable to proceed beyond a certain point. It was as if a wall blocked her path to Simeon, but one she could not see, one that was invisible. When she stretched her hand, she felt nothing, but every repeated effort to get to him was impeded by some unknown barrier.

After a while, she simply stopped trying. She stood there looking helplessly at her son, not sure if he was alive or not. Then she noticed a hazy glow from his foot, his tattoo. She saw that the hazy glow was pulsating as a normal heartbeat. As clearly as she looked on, a stout creature appeared from the corner of the wall and proceeded directly toward her. She could see clearly that it was the tattoo on Simeon's leg. It has taken a life of its own while living within him. She watched as it walked up to Simeon—its face just like Simeon's—turned to look her directly in the eyes as if it knew who she was, then melted into his leg.

She was not sure if she was conscious or dreaming again. She looked at herself, her hands, felt herself, and touched her hair as if to reassure herself that she was still alive. Even then, she was still as confused as she had ever been. Sephinia stood still, gazing so helplessly until the hopelessness of her situation became deeply soaked into her. Then she left and went to her car.

She stood beside her car for several minutes; her feet and much of her dress up to her buttocks were wet. She did not know what to do, and the uncertainty regarding her son was not something she could dismiss. She went back into his apartment.

When she entered the room, she quickly realized that Simeon was no longer where she saw him earlier. She could not even find him anywhere at all. She rushed to the spot where he was; and as she did, she felt she went through a barrier and fell into a different dimension.

From where she landed, she was not able to see the position from where she entered. Where she found herself was cold and had a certain stillness and lifelessness to it. The smell was stale, and she was sickened by the tranquility of the surrounding. *This must be the smell and coldness of death,* she thought.

As her eyes reluctantly searched the room, she could not help but feel uneasy, and the uncanny quietness challenged her consciousness and sanity. She hurried out of the room toward the only exit she could find, and then on to her car. Simeon was standing at the very spot that she was only moments earlier beside her car. "My son, my god, Simeon, what have they done to you?"

She ran toward him, not minding the rain and what then seemed like a flood. She struggled her way to him and wrapped herself around him, touching his face, hair, kissing him as tears pour down her cheeks. "I will get you whatever help you need, my son. Your mother is here. I am with you right here. Whatever it takes to get you right. Don't you worry. I will call Dr. Günther to get us the best help."

With tears still running down her cheeks, she kept stroking her hands over him as if she had just found a long-lost child. "You are not staying here, not any more. You are coming with me, not here." She kept talking like someone out of control.

For what seemed like eternity, no matter how frantic she seemed, Simeon just stood there unfazed and unemotional. His pale countenance defined by a cold, frozen gaze that was void of the least human expression displayed a pair of eyes that did not blink. He seemed as if consciousness deserted him and left an empty, lifeless shell. It was not until after a long while that he responded. It was as if his unconscious body was shocked back into life again; and in a snap, life came back into it. "I am fine, Mother" was all he said, his voice barely audible amid the whaling siren that was enclosed by the sound of rain.

The siren sounded closer and closer as she continued to plead with him to come with her. Then it became clear to her that the police had some interest in that complex when three of their vehicles pulled up in front of the same building that housed Simeon's apartment. But to her surprise, no less than eight officers stepped out of the vehicles toward Simeon and her. "How long have you two been here?" queried one of the officers as the rest surrounded them.

"We have been here for a while. Something I can help you with?" she asked quite calmly.

"Someone left an apartment not too far from here about ten minutes ago after a crime, and I am sorry to say he fits the description. There were other killings also and every eyewitness description seems to be pointing to his direction."

Simeon remained uninterested; and when he did look at the direction of the officer, he did not seem concerned. Even as they stood there, they could hear sirens going on all around town.

"Sir, have you always been at your apartment today?" an officer queried, looking directly at Simeon. They have all either known or heard of him and none of what they have heard or known was pleasant. If they could help it, he would have been gone or disappeared a long time ago. Many have tried, and some were no longer around to tell about their endeavors. In Simeon's terms, those that are gone were harvesters of what they had sown.

As he looked at the officer without blinking and his eyes visibly getting transformed, the officer was getting annoyed at the lack of response to his query. He turned to his mother and said, "Mom, you need to get home so you can dry yourself up." He said the words with the softest voice and a calmness that made his mother abnormally uneasy that she became nervous.

He walked to the driver's side of her car and opened the door. "Come on, mom," he interrupted as she was telling the officer that her son had been asleep in his apartment since she got there, and that she was the one that woke him up.

"I'm sure he can answer that himself. Let's not pretend he's a child that does not understand the question."

She did not like the tone with which the officer made that statement, although she wished that Simeon would simply respond to him so that a flammable situation could be defused. She turned toward his direction as she said, "Just tell him you've been in your apartment sleeping, son." But as she looked at him, she noticed that her son, who was just pale a minute ago, has turned red—too red than normal—and his eyes seemed to emit laser-like rays around the sockets. His pupils had become unnoticeable, perhaps absent altogether.

She became so confused that it seemed she was in the middle of nowhere while everything spun around her. She turned to look at the officers, their hands clutching their guns as she looked from one to the other. A movie scene came to her mind and quickly drifted off.

She turned to look at Simeon again, summing things up in her mind that the outcome would be anything but good. But as she turned to his direction, she noticed a cloud-like formation swirling around him. It would have been a cyclone had it swirled more intensely. Nevertheless, she watched it lazily swirl around and upward. She felt the water getting warm around her feet and the color getting distorted. She almost lost consciousness when she heard her son call in a loud voice, "Mom." It was as if a voice traveled to her from a faraway place. It had an echo about it.

She snapped back into consciousness. "Get into the car." It sounded like an order, and his voice also came amidst those of the officers that were also yelling at him to not move, to put his hands up, to get down.

"Get down now," they continued while they assumed battle positions, guns drawn as if they had encountered a well-armed group that had come to take over the town. Nevertheless, the show of force had one central target, although there was nothing on him that the eyes could see as a weapon.

Before Ms. Rhenoake could intervene further, she became enveloped by the cloud that had suddenly covered a wider space around her and her son. She felt she was no longer on her feet on the solid ground. Inside the cloud, she saw a leaf falling from a very large and tall tree, a mighty Iroko tree. Then a boy drifted up and caught the leaf in midair, then turned and looked at her with a gentle smile. He slowly and gently turned his head the other direction and melted into the cloud.

It was 8:26 early in the evening when Ms. Rhenoake woke up in her own bed, the clothes on her body soaked in cold sweat. She remained seated upright on her bed, gazing at the window with a faint light piercing through the blinds. She sat there, silently debating herself on whether she had a dream or lived a weird reality, something she may never be able to tell anyone if it was real, and one that would not separate her far enough from the realities she has come to know.

She got to her feet, walked into her bathroom, and took off all her clothes. She stood in front of the large mirror in the bathroom with her bare body, but her mind was occupied with series of recent events that she has so far encountered. After a long while, she concluded that a good shower would be soothing enough to help her sleep. She stepped into her shower for a long one. When she was done, she brushed her teeth and poured herself a good glass of wine and laid back down.

When it became obvious that sleep has not invaded, she reached for the phone to call her son. She held the phone for a while, and then put it back down. Whether she was afraid of what she might find out or confirm for herself, she was not sure. She turned on the television instead.

The television screen cleared to reveal what the newscaster said were those that the city lost that day under mysterious circumstances. Among them were photos of five police officers. The newscaster went on to say the officers' bodies were recovered from the parking lot at 334 Kenton Avenue North West. She continued to say that it was not clear what the cause of their deaths was or what led them to the location. She got up and poured herself a larger measure of wine, went to her medicine cabinet, and reached for some capsules. Leaning comfortably on her bed, she gulped down the pills with the wine in her hand, gently rested the glass on her nightstand, and curled up the comforter.

Sephinia felt well rested and energetic when she got up in the morning. She remained there in her bed, sitting up with her knees curled up while thoughts streamed through her mind. She was not sure what to do or how she would start the day. All her thoughts centered on her son even as she found herself rendered indecisive. She gazed at the phone, but the uncertainty of what she might hear or not hear reinforced her reluctance to call. She sat there, trying to make sense of the dream she had. She focused on the similarity of the dream and the event of yesterday that in her mind remained uncertain if it was real or the starting point of what she dreamed later in the night.

It was a cloudy surrounding. The air was cold, not frigid but misty. The misty cloud swirled around lazily as it seemed to move from one direction to the other. It was difficult to make out the ground. The area was surrounded by hills, and she was at the foot of them with the misty, very lazily swirling cloud that had no distinction where it met the heavens.

She was in a long white, long robe that had its hem touching the ground and flared around her as she moved. The sleeves ran the full length of her hands. In front of her was a valley that gently gave out some finer clouds. She could hear the sound of water running down the long valley but could not see it. She could only see the fine, smooth cloud it seemed to bear.

On the other side of the valley across, there was a figure. She could not make out if it was a human figure, but she could hear the cry of a child just from the very spot where it seemed the cloud had formed the shape of a child. It was all white. She could see the "boy" across from her separated by the valley that carried the water she could hear streaming along.

She attempted to walk toward the edge of the valley; but no matter how far she thought she had walked, she still found herself separated by the same distance. Even as she ran for what seemed like a while, the figure was still at the same spot, and she did not seem to advance an inch closer. It seemed she could get a clearer view if she just passed a blotch of cloud. So she felt encouraged to continue, her white robe flaring behind her, and she could feel her heart racing; but it did not seem she made any progress.

As she stood peering at the child's figure and the cry reaching her just as it was before she made the effort to advance further, the cloud above became pierced by sunlight with rays in every direction. It hit her right on her face. She woke up as sunlight came through her window blinds and unto her face, terminating a nightmare she thought lasted for eternity.

After recounting the dream as she sat in her bed with her knees curled up to her chin, she decided to get up and go to her son's apartment. She did not care what comes, what goes, or what happens; she just got to her feet.

When she got to Kenton Avenue, everything seemed normal, except for the yellow tape that secured and barred a certain area from pedestrian traffic. When the door to Simeon's apartment opened, a tired very pale figure emerged to meet his mother. She had never seen him in such a condition since he was born. He looked so fragile and strange, as if something had been feeding off him. He immediately went to lie down on the couch as soon as he had let her in. "I knew you were coming," he muttered. "Did you sleep well?"

"I'm here now," she responded as she sat right next to him. "You seem so out of it, and I hate it. I cannot stand the way you look. I am not interested in asking questions, but I have to get you some help. Whatever it takes, you're all I have."

Her voice was beginning to frail, and tears had already formed around her eyes. She looked around as if she was taking inventory of the things in the room, looking past the several empty water bottles. "Have you eaten? Do you not have anything here to eat?"

"Of course, I do."

"Get on your feet, son. Go, take a warm bath. I will get us something to eat on our way to see Dr. Günther, you hear?"

"Okay, Mom."

"Get on up."

She got up herself and headed to his closet, then came back as he was stretching. She looked him up and down and noticed that his tattooed area was throbbing. It looked red and sore. "I think you might have an infection. That tattoo needs to be checked out. It looks sore, as if it has not yet healed."

As she looked at it, it seemed to be looking back at her. At the time, she thought she saw it blink, but it was the same time she herself blinked.

"Go shower," she reminded as she rested a pair of pants and a long-sleeve shirt on his right shoulder.

"I am Sephinia. Dr. Günther is expecting me," she advised the receptionist at the doctor's office.

"Just a minute, ma'am," the receptionist responded.

"Dr. Günther is ready to see you now," she advised Sephinia as she waved her toward the door where Dr. Günther was waiting.

"Thank you for seeing me in such a short notice, Doctor," Sephinia greeted as they both shook hands.

"Please, have a seat. What can I do for you today?"

Sephinia opened up. She informed Dr. Günther that she had come for the assistance they discussed sometime in the past about her son. She reservedly relayed some of what she had discovered to be out of the normal realm about him. She not only admitted that there was a monumental problem, but she openly asked for whatever help she could get to save her son.

"I am a physician, trained on the use of chemical products to treat problems of the medical nature. However, that is not all there is to sicknesses and illnesses. I consider myself lucky enough to have been trained in a foreign land where it was already understood that all we can see and touch or diagnose and prescribe for are quite minuscule compared to the things we know nothing about.

"There are other types or methods of treatment just as there are other types of illness or sickness. Remember what I told you about why we put the Bible among other reading materials in patient waiting areas? The words in the book may hold the cure for some illnesses for some people. For others, the cure for what ails them may be elsewhere. The only one thing necessary is that the right treatment be administered for a given ailment.

"I would like you to see this man." She hands a piece of paper to Sephinia. It only has a name and a phone number. "He may not hold the cure, but he sure can point you in the right direction. I suggest you call him as soon as you possibly can."

Sephinia did not harbor any hesitation about furthering her quest to secure some help wherever she can get it as long as Simeon's issue gets resolved. When she got into her house, she hurriedly tossed her handbag onto a seat in her living room and headed for the phone.

"I need to speak with Mr. Azark, please."

"It is Adanze that you seek. This is the first messenger." A voice at the other end responded.

"I am Sephinia. I got your number from Dr. Günther. It is about my son. She directed that I contact you about a problem that has come up. You do know Dr. Günther, correct?"

"Can't say that I do, ma'am. It is Adanze that you seek. I am the first messenger."

"It is about my son."

"Go on."

"He was a good boy, very well behaved until he started hanging out with some not-so-well-behaved bunch." Sephinia went on and kept talking nonstop for several minutes. She paused to ask if Mr. Azark was still at the other end.

"Sir, are you there?"

"Go on," he responded.

She continued, "To make this long story short, ever since he got that tattoo, he has never been the same again. It all started immediately after that."

"Do you know how to get here?

"I can find my way."

"Listen very carefully. You are to bring him with you on a Wednesday. It must be a Wednesday of your choice. You must get here before fifteen minutes to midnight but not a second after, Godspeed." The phone went dead.

When Sephinia and her son arrived at Arak shrine, a male dwarf was waiting under a midsize palm tree to meet them. There Simeon was told to take off his footwear. From there on, he became separated from his mother.

Simeon followed the dwarf to an area that looked as strange as what he had seen in his dreams. He was taken to a certain location, motioned not to utter a word, and to stand at a particular spot. The short man walked around him three rounds in one direction, three rounds in the other direction, and stopped right next to the leg that had the tattoo. He proceeded to pull up Simeon's pants to reveal the tattoo. It was throbbing as a bull's heart would. He let down the pants. He then motioned Simeon to follow him.

They came to a stop right beside what looked like a small pond. The water was giving off some steam, yet it was not warm. He motioned him to undress and put his clothes inside a pot made of mud beside him and to not speak. When Simeon had removed his clothes, the short man raised his head. He maintained his gaze at the night sky several minutes as Simeon stood there. The uncanny silence and tranquility of the surrounding was all too abnormal. It was as if the short man was searching the dark, tranquil sky for a sign.

The sky was very calm, and the distant stars were exceptionally tranquil and stationery. When he lowered his head, he immediately motioned Simeon into the pond and, without a word, commanded him to bathe in the water. With his head upward and fixed to the sky, he signaled for him to continue. Simeon remained in the pond for what seemed like a very long time, cleaning his entire body. As he bathed, the water in the pond changed colors and evaporated through thin steam. The short man never looked at his direction but squarely fixed his gaze at the sky, as if he was looking at a stopwatch. When he finally motioned for him to stop with a forceful wave of his hand, he quickly went to a corner in the pond where the remaining small amount of water collected into a boiling swirl. He leaned over with a small calabash, and the water seemed to swirl inside it. He hastily put the lid on.

He motioned Simeon to remain there as he hurried down a path with the calabash in his hand. As he walked, he appeared to be getting shorter and shorter, as if he was going down a steep hill until he disappeared into a bronze cloud of dust. He stood there alone; he could hear the sound of water running down a creek but could not actually see it. The sound of frogs came from a distance. All around, it was so cloudy that he was unable to see past three feet from where he stood. The path that he saw the dwarf walk down with the calabash had become blanketed with stark darkness.

All the while Sephinia was waiting, she remained seated under an *ogirisi* tree, unsure of what would come next. In the chamber of her head, she had relived, many times over, the life of her son as only she could. They had traveled three days to get to this place. "The only agony now is the suspense," she reminded herself. She had dosed off a few times, each time she was awakened by what sounded like waves over the ocean. At times she thought she saw some shadows moving at a distance; nevertheless, she managed to retain some sense of composure.

Suddenly, as she turned in the direction of some noise from behind her, she felt for sure that some things were on the move. It was like a herd of birds walking toward her direction. As they advanced, the daylight dispersed to both sides and quickly transformed into night that behind them was total darkness. Their advance transformed the day into night; every step forward seemed to suck the daylight in front and transformed it into stark darkness behind them.

There was nothing but sandy desert for miles and miles in each direction, yet there was no speck of dust stirred up as the flock of birds approached. When she noticed that the birds had no heads and yet maintained their formation as they advanced, she thought she was once again dreaming. She lowered her head and hid her face in the shelter of her knees.

Closer and closer, the sound came as that of a stampede as it came from all around her. She maintained her eyes tightly closed solely out of fear. The sound became even more intense, as if thousands of soldiers marched around her. Suddenly, daylight, as she remembered it the last time she had her eyes open, was gone. Darkness had overtaken daylight.

Unexpectedly, tranquility prevailed, and it all became very, very calm. A certain cold wind descended all around her. It was so dark, she could not even see the very knees she rested her head on.

As she sat there not knowing what would come next, next to her ear came a voice.

"*You have sought Adanze. I am the first messenger. Bear ye these words well into thy ears. What ails your lad is not of this land. For the deeds afar, the souls of the wronged have come for vengeance. Many have, and more will be afflicted, even the ones unintended and the unborn. The ghosts of many a soul have declined to sleep. Night and day, their spirits hover and wail. Night and day, the wombs that nurtured them twist and ask for vengeance. They lay offerings at the shrine and wish ill on them that despised their worth. The very land of theirs stands defiled. The native soil void of her worth, for Satan has descended and abomination now abound. In a faraway land lies some hope. Far and wide, he must journey to the land of her that time forgot, where the dead dwell with them that live and the night and day separated only by a shadow.*

"*Seven towns and seven rivers he must journey, for his ills are not of this land. Vengeance has come. Children will demise those that bore them while friends murder friendship. In the hands of men, their wives will perish, for the ills meted on other lands, the wind returns one fruit from the nest. The desecrator of their land has assumed ownership and comes and goes as such. Seventh night from hence the path is revealed, for he must journey, or the soul is forsaken. Fare thee well."*

Without warning, daylight descended, casting brightness all around her; and although she had her eyes closed, she sensed and felt it. Without further suspense, she opened her eyes. She looked around her as if to reassure herself that it was not a dream; but she just could not be sure that it was not. As she turned to her right, she saw Simeon walking toward her as the dwarf stood at a distance looking toward her direction.

"What happened there?" she asked as she stood up and wrapped her hands around him. "Are you all right? Did anything happen to you? What happened?"

"I only remember walking with him to a pond in a garden-like area. I remember being led right into the pond and being in a corner surrounded by the sound of running water with deafening croaks of frogs. I could not remember anything else until he led me out of the narrow entrance where leaves of plants in another garden turned away from our direction."

Just as they walked a few steps away from where she had waited under a tree, she casually glanced back. She noticed that a large bird was circling the tree in a continuous motion. She thought it was odd how it got there so quickly without a sound. She took a few steps back toward the tree only to see that the bird did not have a head, yet it continued its march around the tree without missing a step. It was the size of a guinea fowl, but of specie she had never seen or known. "Let us hurry out of here," she told her son hurriedly.

Sephinia was just about to leave the drugstore one evening when she looked up at the television only to see the picture of Simeon all over the screen. She had just finished paying for some sleeping pills she had picked up. It has become rather difficult for her to fall asleep at night; and when she managed to close her eyes, it was no more the sleep as she knew it. Her mind regularly drifted everywhere that it even became dreadful falling asleep. The picture on the television had "suspect" captioned under it but was barely audible. She quickly left the store and headed to her car. As she hurriedly entered her house, she reached for the remote control and turned on the television.

There had been another murder; and as Sephinia listened, she gathered that seven people were gruesomely murdered at a party the previous night but was not discovered until later in the day. As she continued to listen, the reporter said that the bodies were ripped open with some internal organs taken out of the bodies. Some had their eyes gouged out, jaws torn apart, and two of them had their tongues pulled out. The report continued that some police officers have been sent to look for the suspect based on some eyewitness accounts. She hurriedly left her house and headed for her son's apartment, not minding to turn off the television.

When she reached Kenton Avenue Northwest, she saw the entire complex surrounded by what she thought was the military just waiting for the order to start a war. Nevertheless, she was told they were the police and motioned to not get any closer.

As she stood there wondering the whereabouts of her son, an officer came running to his colleagues that were waiting between some of the squad cars and the yellow tape. "No one in there, but there was something quite strange. When officer Lemke and I breached the entrance, there was no one in the room. The floor was wet. And as we rushed in, all the water on the floor collected itself in one spot. Right before our eyes, the water moved toward the entrance door. And in a blink, it gave out this bright, blinding flash, and then it vanished," he narrated.

"Where is Officer Lemke?"

"He just stood there. I could not."

About five of them rushed to the room. Officer Lemke was still standing there. He could no longer see. He went blind and unable to speak. He could only lazily move his head from left to right. They led him out and into a waiting ambulance. His senses were gone.

All the people that gathered were staring with heightened curiosity. Without warning, a very strong cold wind descended all around the whole area. It was strong enough that it left the entire area swept clean of leaves and debris, then carefully navigated them to the graveyard at the Church of Saint Mark right beside a tombstone. Like a mountain, the debris towered over the area that it was visible from a distance. Below that mountain of debris stood a tombstone with the name "Marcus" carved on it.

The city was in uproar. People flocked to the church to bear witness to the unusual, strange occurrence. Many went into the church to pray and ask for a revelation, for answers, for some explanation. Many more—and some that attended services at the church—swore to never go near there ever again.

To many more, it became the confirmation of the story that had swirled around the town for some time. Some that have passed by the graveyard on foot at night and early in the mornings have heard the cries of little children coming from there. Some reported seeing little children walking up and down the graveyard early before dawn. Others narrate how they narrowly missed running over some children crossing the road at night only to not see them after their vehicles had screeched to a stop.

Marcus was a soldier who spent a lot of time in foreign lands where he was a part of many ungodly acts that prevailed for some time. Many, of whom most were children, perished in his hands and in the hands of those of his kind as part of what they were sent to do.

The surviving parents of those he saw to their deaths prayed to their gods to avenge the lives of their children. Some collectively went and made offerings at various oracles and shrines, demanding vengeance in accordance with their values. Some personal belongings of those that died—including their pictures, clothes, and hair—were left at the oracle shrines, and they demanded that vengeance be exerted.

Seven months, seven weeks, seven hours, and the seventh minute after Marcus came back, he killed his mother, wife, and his three children before taking his own life. However, the first thing he did after he came back home was that he went out and got himself a tattoo. He carved his left arm with the stinging tail of a scorpion. It was his first outing following his return from serving those whose comfort he sought to protect in his misguided thought he was doing something noble.

Before he went overseas where he committed untold savagery, he regularly attended services at Saint Mark where he received his sacrament of baptism and Holy Communion. To many, he seemed a devout Christian, and so his burial at the church's cemetery only seemed fitting for what was deemed an uncommon devotion to Christianity in general and Catholicism in particular. That was the common information that prevailed around town about him. At his burial ceremony, his eulogy nearly conferred on him sainthood if only it was allowed without some miracle, real or imagined.

When Sephinia became convinced that Simeon was not in his apartment, she decided to go back to her house. She did not have to travel far before she came to an abrupt stop at a four-way intersection. To the left corner of the street were five freshly decapitated bodies with blood running down the street. As she blinked to reassure herself of what she had just seen, a human torso landed in the middle of the intersection, blood gushing out of it.

She lost it, pushed the gas pedal as hard as she could, and propelled her Buick past the street toward her house, not minding the road or traffic condition. She would stop again soon afterward when she noticed Simeon come out of the bush and quickly went into the other side of the street into the bush. His speed of crossing was faster than could ever be humanly possible.

"Simeon," she shouted in a surprising but cautious tone. "Simeon, it's your mother."

He turned to look in her direction. His eyes appeared very dark and his face off-color that it startled his mother.

She could hear her own heartbeat as it pounded against her chest. "Come on, son. You can come home now. Come with me. Let me get you some help." She was out of the car with the door ajar. "They are looking for you, Simeon. Please do not waste time. Come with me."

Right before her eyes, she watched as his eyes, hair, and skin transformed into his normal feature. "Let us go home," she pleaded with tears in her eyes, helpless and unsure of everything but wholly defeated by the bond between mother and child. With shaky hands, she walked up to him, wrapped her arms around him, and guided him into the car. As they headed to her house, they passed several police vehicles passing by them at high speeds, heading in every direction with sirens blaring. Tears poured down her eyes as she drove in silence.

On getting to her house, Simeon appeared deeply weakened, his now yellowish eyeballs deep into their sockets and blood dripping out of his nostrils. His mother went into a panic as she heard him plead for water in a tone that was barely audible. She quickly ran to the kitchen, held a plastic cup to the faucet and ran to get him the water.

He lay his body flat on the floor while he pleaded for more and more water. His mother ran back and forth, to and from the kitchen. By the time the situation normalized, Simeon had gulped more than a gallon of water. With his body fully hydrated, his eyes no longer seemed sunk, and he calmly drifted into sleep. But just as his mother thought she could put herself together, her eyes found themselves rested on his tattoo; and as she looked at it pounding as if it was his heart beating, the figure that was the tattoo grew right before her eyes. As she remained captivated by fear, her throat very dry, the figure looked more and more like her son, transformed into a creature that stepped out of his body, and then melted into a pool of water. Her mouth was wide open, but there was no sound coming from her. She slumped backward and passed out.

Sephinia listened attentively as a tiny female figure stood in front of her and called her attention. The tiny figure was giving her some instructions, and she felt she needed to pay attention to understand what it was about. The voice began,

"The time has come, and it is now.

"The one you seek is Adanze. I am the second messenger. Morrow the curfew tolls for the path that will lead to her. The path is rough, and where it ends, I know not, for the one you seek is she that time forgot. Seek ye first the oil of the ancient from the land of the lost tribe that thy feet may tremble but not wither, that he can see but not be blinded, and journey back from whence he touched. The call is now, and your journey has begun.

"Morrow at sunset you shall rise. You must not look back once your step is maiden, for what you may see could blind your eyes. What you

may hear, your ears may not shelter, lest the ants feed on him that feels but bound acast.

"*You shall proceed eastward with him at the left of your shadow but afore. Eastbound at sunset, ye shall continue even as the things around you wither, even as you are dwarfed by the things around you and unsure of them if alive or dead. Remain ye steadfast, for every step shall yield the less of him that you know, and eastbound ye shall continue until you see no more of him.*

"*Then shall ye turn and proceed west, never to look back east until thy sun rises. For ye shall see the sun rise from the west, and when it has risen, then shall ye find yourself in your nest until this message is renewed.*

"*Fare thee well. At sunset, your feet shall be eastbound, for that is thy rise.*"

All the while, Sephinia was unable to clearly see the tiny female's face no matter how hard she tried to focus in. When she had finished, she simply broke into tiny pieces of dust; and with a high-pitched sweeping sound, the dust looked like it was forcefully swept away in one direction. The sound pushed the dust toward her face; and as she waved her hand to give herself some breathing space, her hand hit the end of the couch beside her.

She woke up. She remained there for some time, her mind very busy as she struggled to confirm to herself that it was indeed that seventh day. The message stuck to her head very vividly. She resigned to not query herself for too long. She got the message. "It is that time. It is now," she soliloquized.

Even as she was set to get herself ready for what she termed in her mind "the trip to the abyss," she remained puzzled and preoccupied. Not minding whatever uncertainty she was surrounded by, she got to her feet. She looked to confirm that Simeon was still asleep. She did not want to disturb him, although she was not too concerned as she invested all her hopes that she was about to get him back from whatever it was that was trying to wrestle him away from her and away from normal existence. With her handbag hanging from her shoulder, she left the house.

As Simeon lay there seemingly in deep sleep, a tall and thin man with gray hair appeared to him with a bowl in his hand. Simeon could not see what was inside the bowl. The man approached slowly toward him through a cloudy path.

He appeared to have been clothed in long leather coat that covered from his neck down to his heels. His eyes bore wrinkles that suggested that time has not dealt kindly with him. His pointed nose was like a cone, and his face was a testament to the effects of time.

As the man stood in front of him, Simeon could hear him speaking but his lips did not move. The more his words came to Simeon, the more forceful they reverberate, inducing him that his problem was his mother and that he permanently separate from her. He was forcefully urging him to kill his mother.

> "For while she breathes, your life a misery and existence cursed,
> Immense suffering your fate, and your plea for own demise a wish.
> Render her a corpse that thy freedom is restored by thy hands.
> Take the sword to her heart and be redeemed in the sacrifice."

More and more forceful and demanding were his words, and he felt his thoughts were becoming less and less stable. The more the tall, thin figure talked, the more the color of his face changed. He was now paler than he appeared before. And when some steam started coming out of his nose, Simeon stood up and stretched his hand toward him. The man opened his mouth and a glittering sword came out. He pulled it out and handed it to Simeon and slowly bowed his head.

But as Simeon turned around to where he last saw his mother, she was not there. He slowly lowered the sword as he turned to the old man. He was no longer there. He just let go of the sword as a noise woke him up. Sephinia had just closed and locked the door after her.

"I need just one minute with Dr. Günther, please. She asked me to come," she lied to the receptionist at the doctor's office.

"I will let her know you're here, ma'am," the receptionist pledged as she made her way toward the doctor's office.

"Sephinia, I do not remember—"

"I know, Dr. Günther," she interjected. "I had to lie to her in order to see you for just a minute."

"Okay?"

"Would you have any idea what in the world the ancient oil from the land of the lost tribe means?"

"Oil of the ancient from the land of the lost tribe. That is a certain type of palm oil found only in the land of the lost tribe. The lost tribe dwells in the center and origin of the earth where the longitude and latitude begin. The oil comes from different species of palm trees. Either it is only found there or that it has its origin in the dwelling place of the lost tribe.

"It is known as "Akwu Ojukwu." It is visibly different from the rest of the palm nuts found around the world. The oil from it is different as a result of that difference in its specie. It is rare, very rare. Legend has it that it is a cure for many diseases and neutralizes even poison if the right amount is administered early enough. It is also said to ward off or cast away evil spirits.

"What about it, though?"

"It is about Simeon. I need to get my hands on that oil."

"The only place in this town I can think of is the Rare & Essentials store in Okuzu. It won't be cheap if they have it. Try there. I have a patient waiting for me."

"I must be heading there. Thank you, Dr. Günther."

"Good luck."

"I need it. Thank you."

Back at her house, she came in as Simeon was helping himself through some water, gulping it down as if he had been living in the desert for a century. He laid down again and quickly fell into deep sleep. As the depth of his sleep deepened, he felt he was being pulled by some powers into a deeper state until he saw himself in front of the thin, slim man again. And as soon as they faced each other, he immediately opened his mouth and pulled out the same sword and quickly handed it to Simeon. At the same time the man bowed his head or gave a nod to him, Simeon had barely turned around when a loud wail enveloped the cave-like surrounding. He instinctively turned around only to see the man vomiting blood, his ears bulging out and more blood coming through his nose and eyes as he wailed.

Since Sephinia concluded she could not just let him go to sleep again without some intervention, she forced some of the palm oil into his mouth and proceeded to generously rub some over his legs and heels. She was more generous on the amount she doused over his tattoo. She thought it was interesting that as soon as she rubbed the oil over the tattoo, his flesh began to twitch, and the tattoo bubbled as if something was fighting from the inside to get out. His skin bulged out and sunk in repeatedly. *The demon wants out,* she thought to herself.

After a while, it quieted down, sort of, but it kept throbbing. She applied more of the oil and sat down to rest. Although she had not eaten for a very long time, the feeling of hunger was still absent. She sank more comfortably in the couch with the jar containing the palm oil right next to her. She had decided to get some rest while she waited for something of which she was not sure.

She looked up to see the person in front of her. She was a tiny female, no taller than forty-six inches. She was dressed in a gray overall, and her head was completely wrapped in a scarf reminiscent of a certain religious dress code. The scarf was of similar color, and only her face was visible.

She noticed that Simeon was also present. The dwarf pointed both of them to a direction without saying a word. All around hung a yellow cloud, and all Sephinia knew was that other things, perhaps people, were moving to and from both sides of them. No matter how hard she tried to distinctively make out if they were humans or not, her efforts were not successful.

As time passed, she became convinced that the moving figures were men and women all wrapped in their clothing. She noticed that they all moved independent of each other. It was as if she and Simeon were not there because not one of those that moved on each side of them looked in their direction or did anything to acknowledge their presence. The female dwarf followed right behind them as they maintained a steady pace.

They walked for quite a distance, at least that was how it seemed to Sephinia, when all of a sudden, without any prior advice or directive, a towering shadow overtook them. It swept from their left side and drifted in front of them. As it did, it felt as if they both stepped down onto a lower elevation. Her gut feeling was that the dwarf was no longer behind them, but she was too afraid to look back. She felt so uneasy and anxious for not knowing what was going on behind them. *"From hence you go on, never to look back until it is time. The one you seek is Adanze,"* the dwarf told them.

They continued on their path for what seemed like days and nights, but the weather never changed. Night never came, although they had no means of knowing the time. Others passed by them on both sides. Some she thought to be men, others with their heads covered in scarves she assumed to be women. There were more that she thought were mothers holding their babies to their chests. All around them, from the ground to as high as she could see, it was the color of a sandy desert void of clarity and clouded with dust. She was unable to see the faces of any that they passed or of those that passed them.

They kept on walking at the same pace, but the scenery began to change. They came across what she thought were vultures standing on the sides. For every short distance, they came across one, and then they began to see some birds as big as ducks walking on both directions. Some were coming while others were going.

As they kept on, they came across some large birds that were circling a tiny dusty cyclone. She noticed that the birds had no heads, but they all stopped to turn toward their direction as if they saw them passing by. As they continued on, she noticed she could make out the blue and gray clouds farther ahead of them. They continued as she noticed the gray and blue clouds sort of foam and bubble in and out of each other, like objects in conflict.

As they walked on, she could hear the sound of a bell coming somewhere from their right side with a faint voice she could not quite make out. They continued at their pace for just a short distance farther when a cold wave swept through them. It was as if the wave carried with it the sound of a bell and a voice that was short of clarity.

Right ahead of them, she noticed a graveyard suspended in the middle of the air. It was like an island in the middle of the air. Up there was a man dressed in a red robe with a bell in his hand. There were tombstones around him as he walked from one direction to the other. He held the bell in his right hand while he pointed and made gestures with his left. He rang the bell repeatedly and made his incantations. The voice began to gain more and more clarity as she watched him pointing to one direction, and he said.

> *"Look yonder. Under that marble stone, he dwells.*
> *For many, he was the son of darkness,*
> *For never was he content within his land*
> *He stole. He killed and raped the ones afar.*
> *Death, destruction, and evil his gift to other lands,*
> *A mighty warrior he once was passing through time.*
> *For those without a soul, he stood a hero*
> *As they triumph in the blood of the innocent."*

Sephinia could now hear the man very clearly and distinctively. She was also able to see he wore a long black beard accented by gray lines that covered his cheeks and chin. She watched him move to another side of the graveyard and continued as he rang the bell while pointing to a direction, as if he was showing someone a particular set of graves among others and describing the dead that dwell within.

> *"Beneath those marbles of fancy lay the*
> *Remains of fools that once lived,*
> *The sheep that questioned not the lies*
> *Drenched by Satan while mothers dared not reason.*
> *Time and again a satanic tool they'd been.*
> *And for him with conscience, they stand despised*
> *As they lay there forever dead and eternally silent,*
> *For those they violated, their souls they curse."*

She reasoned that the man might have been telling a story based on actual events, or that he was issuing some warnings that others ought to give some ear to. But the way he dedicatedly moved from one grave to the other, each with its own headstone, she also considered that the man must be a prophet issuing some warning to those that have ears of the lessons of yesterday in order to prepare them for the tomorrow that is to come. Shaking his head from left to right he continued,

> "Oh, how blind we seem to history, how dismissive.
> In pretense, we proclaim as good the evils of time.
> The split-tongued snakes of history ever untamed
> As they remain no less the sons of their fathers."

After they had walked for what seemed like six more hours, she noticed the blur ahead of them has been removed as she witnessed a stream of mirage swept by, and the suspended graveyard vanished. Then she saw that a figure far ahead was waving them on. It was a short dark figure continuously waving them on as they trekked.

Suddenly, the figure vanished, but they walked on; and as they did, she noticed that Simeon was now getting ahead of her even though they walked at the same pace. The gap between them widened with him gaining more and more distance ahead of her. Moreover, as he gained more distance and left her farther behind, he seemed to be getting more and more diminished in physical stature and size. It progressed to the point that after a while, she could no longer see him. It seemed he disappeared into a thick darkness. And as she tried to advance farther, she was no longer able to do so; and although she could not feel any physical barrier, she was simply unable to advance any further no matter how hard she tried. She decided it was time to turn around.

Gripped with fear of what she might be faced with upon turning around, she closed her eyes as she made the turn. She became wrapped with uncertainty when it became obvious to her that just seconds ago behind her, there was stark darkness. And now that she was westbound, it was daylight. She wondered if her position was the boundary between light and darkness. She wondered if she herself, not necessarily her position, were the boundary bridging both. She maintained her composure, bearing in mind the instructions and warnings from the messengers thus far.

As she remained westbound, it was a completely different environment. Although she and her son passed the same route eastbound, or so she thought, going back the same route westbound was markedly different. The scene was different, and her movement was anything but normal. It seemed that as she walked, the things around her moved, but she did not gain any distance. Nevertheless, she kept on westbound.

From the horizon, she could see what amounted to an apparition. Simeon lay stretched out on a mat, and a woman was seated beside him and was administering palm oil on his feet. Sephinia could hear the female as she gave instructions to a third person standing directly opposite her. She could not tell much about the person, only that he or she wore a long robe that covered the entire body to the ground.

"*You must provide him a sword that he may stand in defense of himself,*" the lady said. "*A spear, bows and arrows, seven calabashes of water set aside for him that he may never thirst. Some dried bread of oat and a jar of honey, lest he hunger. Some of those boxes to his left, more to his right, that uncertainty never overcomes him, and seven of you to remain guard that his needs are met as he journeys to her that time forgot. Adanze is the one he needs, for the devil in him has assumed his body and acts at will. Rise, ye all, and prepare him for where he must journey, to the shared land of the dead and the living.*"

Sephinia observed and heard everything as if she was in a theatre watching a show. While she continued westbound, she noticed that the sky ahead of her was beginning to change. The sky began to resemble that of an early morning sunrise. The cloud movements gave way to the piercing rays of the sun rising from the west. *What an anomaly,* she thought. She understood she was not to look back under any circumstance, but nonetheless could not help but wonder if there was something or someone following right behind her.

Suddenly, the apparition reappeared. Sephinia saw that seven figures all dressed in robes were sitting around Simeon while the woman stood speaking to them.

"This is not a journey of the temporal. Therefore, before his departure, he must be well prepared. For he may never come back if he is ill prepared. He must know that everything he would ever need is here, and that you are all available to provide assistance as the need is called for. When he gets to the waters of separation, you are to see that he crosses over safely. The food and everything else he would need have been gathered, and what have been put together are more than he would need for the seven-day journey. His shield is the best that ever existed. Which one of you here is unfit to make this journey? Which one of you is unwilling? For it is in order for the unwilling or the unfit to retreat. But if there is not a discontent, then shall you bow your heads that the incense may be lit."

The seven figures that were dressed in robes bowed their heads. At the instant that they did, the woman raised what looked like a lamp made of wire mesh to a burning candle. Light "jumped" over to the lamp as if it simply magnetized the energy. The lamp gave out a huge thick cloud of smoke in all directions; and as the smoke circled the area, Sephinia found herself drawn toward the scene of the apparition with each step she made until she suddenly found herself standing in one end. She was now inside and among them. *"Find you at rest, for the sunrise is now."* She heard the sound come from the short woman, but her mouth did not move as the words came unto her.

Sephinia sank herself into the big weird-looking seat, the only one left in the area she could not quite call a room. It was more like a stage suspended in the middle of nothing, more like a plate suspended in the middle of the air. That was what it seemed like before she entered into it. However, when she found herself in it, she could not see anything else other than those and things around. No sooner than she was seated did the area get brighter and brighter; the sun became visible to her just as it would rise on any normal day. "It is sunrise." She said to herself.

As the sun became more and more visible, as it does every normal day, Sephinia became convinced that although it looked like any normal day, it appeared too close and its energy too intense, at least in appearance. It soon became apparent to her that as the sun approached, their immediate surrounding was in motion. With every advance of the sun, she noticed that they were in motion advancing forward. However, it seemed that instead of them moving, things on both sides of them were moving past them. It was not long when she discovered that they were in what she understood to be a town.

On both sides of them, and as far ahead as she could see, there was nothing but barren flat solid surface punctuated by what seemed like trees with leafless branches. There were some unusually tall, dead or dying cactus plants with branches that accented the vast area. The surface, or what seemed to be the ground, was covered with white matter while the trees and their branches stuck out in all directions. The surface looked stale and void of air.

From her position, she summed up that the area is not capable of supporting animal life. As far as she was concerned, it seemed against nature that trees and the brownish dried-up cacti ever thrived on it. The scene was the same for miles and miles, repeating itself as if they were going in circles. The vastness of the area and its barren nature conveyed nothing to her other than the aura of lifelessness.

She imagined that there might have been life on it, but perhaps tragedy engulfed the vast area, leaving it in the current condition. The things she could not reconcile, as far as nature is concerned, are some phenomena she observed.

The more she scanned the area with her heightened curiosity, the more she discovered some abnormalities. She could not make sense as to how it was possible that plants pierce through the surface and spring out some branches right before her eyes. That was exactly one of the occurrences she witnessed. The plants and their branches remained there fully grown to their short full statures with their leafless, dried-up branches sticking out in all directions.

She wondered about the different species of the cacti that scattered over the vast space. The sight of albino cacti preyed enormously on her curiosity. She admired the beauty she found in them, especially how they appeared with their purple-colored thorns that dotted the blades. Despite the random beauty that brightened her mood, she nevertheless concluded that a messenger of death still hovered over the vast area. The scene was the same, and she never noticed anything different until they came unto a river—or the river came unto them.

It was a river of molten gold, flowing lazily like thick molten lava. It seemed as if the energy from the sun had melted the world's gold and turned it into a flowing ocean. From their position, she thought that they ought to be feeling enormous amount of heat; however, there was no air or anything else but the river of molten gold that randomly revealed some sparkling glitter on its surface.

For a while, that was all that drifted alongside them until they came unto an area where Sephinia noticed some intense lightning streaks. It repeatedly came from the depth of the clouds, piercing through and striking the surface of the river with unfathomable energy with which it pushed through its thickness. Each time it struck, it generated a tremendous tremor that temporarily destabilized the surrounding, which quickly healed itself just for another strike to take place.

As some of the flashes hit the surface, canals are created, only to hurriedly seal themselves, and the flow continued. As each bright light came down, it revealed a surface that boiled just as an extremely hot pot of custard, shooting off what she assumed must be hot bubbles so high they rained back onto the surface.

The molten river, with its own atmospheric surrounding, looked more like a planet onto itself. Sephinia was overly preoccupied with comparing the scene she was looking at to the sun that she has known in her real world. She disagreed with her subconscious that it would be impossible for lightning to be visible in the middle of the sun. She thought to herself, *If that were to occur, no eye will survive the sight to see ever again.*

But as they drifted on, or as things drifted past them, her sight was drawn toward a large canal that was just created by another lightning strike. Her jaw dropped open in awe of what she had noticed. As she remained wrapped in astonishment, wondering if what she saw was indeed a line of humanlike creatures with loads on their heads walking inside the canal before it sealed up.

The same streak of powerful light struck again at the spot on the surface, once again revealing some human-looking figures, all walking in the same direction, carrying what seemed to her like some pots made of clay. The pots were big, and the creatures were void of hands. It seemed to her that the particular light that repeatedly struck that same spot was timed and occurred about every seven seconds.

As far and wide as she could see, it was nothing but a river of molten gold. She moved her head away from looking at the scene. She rubbed her eyes with both her palms, perhaps just to reassure herself that things are still real, that she was not at all insane but rather very much normal.

For the few seconds she rubbed and opened her eyes, the vast river of gold had disappeared. She found themselves in a town. This was the second town they had come into, and it seemed to be something out of the norm. The land was gray and had no sign of life to the best of her assumption. Hovering, over it was an object Sephinia assumed to be the moon for its surface.

The object was visibly spinning in a lazy manner, casting a grayish shadow over the surface. She could not make out if they were close or far from it. The grayish illumination coming from it over the surface was not at all welcoming. She saw it as a different planet that altogether had its own moon but not a sun to brighten things up and perhaps give life. *This has nothing to offer humanity,* she thought to herself. She concluded that there must be a story about a place like that. She wondered if there could be people present somewhere that kept a history of what happened there that left it the way it appeared. She thought of it as a cold, stale town if it is indeed not a planet of its own.

For a split second, it seemed they passed under a shade, or that a shadow passed over them. It was a thin dark shade that she noticed very suddenly went over them. She did not see it coming, but she was sure it either passed over them or they passed under it. The very moment she experienced it, her attention drifted to the left of their position onto a very dark body of water that seemed to flow very violently alongside them. It was like an ocean of crude oil with a violent and turbulent flow.

It was a huge body of water so wide there was nothing else visible past it. Despite its size and the force with which it drifted, there was not a sound from the river. Sephinia kept looking at the manner the river was moving, forming ridges that slammed against themselves. As she watched, it occurred to her that she never really saw the beginning of the river; and as far as her eyes could see, there was no end to it. All she did was look in the direction, and there it was.

It then dawned on her that she could not tell much about the first town they passed through, when or where it ended, and where the first river began. No cloud, no sky, no horizon—just pure darkness and a sudden leap void of any defined border. And it seemed quite odd that despite the ridges of the water slapping very forcefully and violently against itself, there was not a sound she could hear. What boggled her mind even more was that when she looked to the right where there was once a town, there was nothing there but stark darkness. There was nothing beyond that darkness; or to put it in another term, there was nothing for her to see beyond the darkness. No cloud, no sky, no horizon—just pure darkness. Then her gaze shifted to Simeon.

She noticed that there were some calabashes of water by Simeon's feet. There was a circle made with palm oil that formed a ring behind the seven people that encircled him. She then noticed that the tattoo on his foot had stretched his skin and stood about a foot upright. It seemed to be wrestling to get out of his skin and onto the surface. Its eyes were cast directly at her, as if it was beckoning for some assistance. She remembered his friends once told her they called the character Zeus and how they had seen it blink right there from Simeon's foot; and when they spoke of it, they were ridiculed by their friends.

To her greatest surprise, she saw Zeus blink just as she stared it down with abundant, unmitigated disdain. It was at that moment that she realized that she herself could not blink. When she wanted to wink as a display of her revulsion of Zeus, her eyelids could not move. It was at that time that she realized that she had not blinked since she found herself on the present scene of her journey to reclaim her son. To her, Zeus is the evil that has taken over her son, assumed his entire being, and has commanded his actions ever since. She had so many questions, but there was no one to ask. She would like so many answers, but no one had them. It had dawned on her that she was helpless; now the helplessness has been compounded by hopelessness, and it is all weighing heavily on her maternal consciousness.

Within the split second she took her eyes off and decided to get her thoughts off to a different direction, whichever that might be, the dark ocean had vanished. The surprise she felt made her a bit startled. Once again, there was no sign of where the water ended. It was just as if what she knew as the present was instantly blanketed with a new reality without a boundary separating the end of one and the beginning of the other. She found herself in another town that is completely different and bore no resemblance to anything that bordered an ocean of starkly dark water.

This town was markedly different. If for nothing else, it had some life in it. They seemed to be passing through the middle of it because there were things on both sides, unlike others that they had passed, or those that passed them. There were birds of different sizes walking on both sides. The soil or ground as she could see it was reddish. Trees were sparse, and no matter the size, each was capped with a large colorful leaf. There was not a tree with branches or more than a leaf, although there seemed to be varieties; however, they all have one thing in common: each was capped with what appeared to be a large wide leaf of varied colors.

When her attention deviated from the trees, it centered on the birds to their right. They moved in straight lines and moved only in two directions, forward or the opposite direction in a very organized manner. One size in a line of birds within the link punctuated those of other sizes.

It had been calm and smooth so far as they journeyed until they were shaken by what seemed like a tremor. It was as if the wind swept through under them. It was then that she wondered if there was anything touching the ground from where they were, although she recalled that it appeared like an apparition suspended in midair when she first noticed it. It was like a plate or sheet suspended in the air with occupants on it, but that was before she found herself drawn in and become a part of it. All it took was just a sudden, unanticipated sway that startled her and thus rattled her state of mind when she found herself on it.

As she glanced to her left, she noticed that the birds on that side were no longer on the march. She quickly looked to the right and noticed the same thing. The birds were gathering in circular forms, all facing the same direction. Her eyes rested on a neatly organized, well-manicured, and orderly groomed graveyard with elegant tombstones that seemed to beckon death even for them that still yearn for life.

As they journeyed on, her eyes came to rest on a flock of birds moving in opposite directions. She stared at them when she noticed that when each set of two walked into each other, the two became one bird, then immediately turned and walk in the opposite direction. *This is one strange town,* she thought to herself. As they came to where some of the strange trees stood in a cluster, all the birds from the left and right of them turned to look their direction. She heard, in a very clear and distinctive tone, a voice saying,

> "Once, a son on whom much was bestowed,
> One mother without a voice, and a son demised,
> In silence time has, for many, trammeled misfortune.
> And the devil is never without a dagger.
> Nine months and labor a sacrifice to a false god.
> In the quest for blood, a mother's right a null.
> With a devil of many tongues, the truth of late
> And a godly gift is transformed a satanic tool."

Just as it all went silent and calmness descended, darkness also descended and engulfed around them. It was the first time she had seen darkness engulf them since she found herself in the midst. Then she heard the sound of moving water reminiscent of a waterfall. The sound became louder as they proceeded, although she was still not sure if they were moving forward or that things moved past them.

She noticed a faint light ahead. It appeared very tiny as it flickered like an open flame quite a distance ahead of them. Every advance of the light came with a sound reminiscent of a waterfall. The closer the light appeared, the louder the sound of the waterfall.

It was not long before the things around them began to wobble. As time went on, what started as a mere vibration became more like an earthquake. Things tumbled over, and the men around Simeon struggled to remain seated. Amid the increasing sound of waterfall came moans from the area where Simeon was positioned. When Sephinia looked in that direction, she noticed that while the men around Simeon struggled to remain seated, Zeus's stature stretched out from the inside of his skin as if to escape his body and come out onto the surface. It seemed to have been one of the most bizarre experiences she has come to endure. It rendered her into more uncertainty, and she became even more restless.

The flickering light steadily made its way toward them to the point that they could see around their immediate area. But beyond the immediate surroundings, there was stark darkness, and it was only that tiny light that cast some reflections against what appeared to be hailstones that rained on both sides of them with the sound of a gigantic waterfall.

Sephinia had initially thought the sound came from the flow of a big body of water moving at a very fast pace. She never expected it would be hailstones raining down so violently that it caused immense vibration around them. With the deafening noise, it continued raining hailstones for a very long time, causing almost everything around them to tumble over until it suddenly stopped without a sign of waning. As it ended, the tiny light transitioned into a full blast of the sun. It was daylight once again in a town.

This is a town without life. There was nothing in it that gives off any sign of life anywhere in its vastness. As they journeyed on, or as things went past them, it seemed like a desert of salt or off-white earth as far as Sephinia could see.

From her position, she could see something she passed as reflection of light or heat. There were mirages, each melting away as another came into view. She noticed that there was nothing to the left side of them but black stark darkness. To her, it seemed as if the left side of them was against a wall without a space in between. It seemed unusually strange to her as she noted that in front and well ahead of them, she could see as far from the left as she could from the right; but as they moved forward, or things moved past them, there was nothing but darkness from the beginning of the area they were in. She wondered how such a large expanse of what could still be called land was so barren with not even a single sign of a plant or grass. She mentally punctuated the area with Joshua trees and cacti, but she recognized that such would be very out of place. *How could anyone justify anything green on this type of surface?* she queried herself inaudibly.

As they journeyed on, although it seemed more like they drifted on or space drifted past them, Sephinia began to see what she believed to be some objects in motion. Far ahead and to the right of them, she could see some shiny objects but was not quite able to make out what they were. From where she was seated, the objects appeared to be moving, some moving farther to the right while others moved to the left.

The closer they got, the more she noticed that the objects moved in a somewhat strange manner. Rather, every motion was like that of a heartbeat and advanced with each pulse. For a very long time the scene remained just like that, and the distance seemed to have frozen in time without any farther advance.

Then, in what seemed like a flash in time, rows and rows of tombstones came into view with glistening steam hovering around them. As far into the distance as she could see, there was no end. She could swear they were surrounded by the smell of death with ghosts hovering over what she termed the "field of the dead."

"But where are the people who buried the dead in those graves? What happened to them, and from whom is the sound coming?" she kept asking herself questions one after another as everything seemed frozen. She felt that things have been suspended in time. She could not move any of her body parts, and everyone around her also seemed frozen in time or immobilized. All she could do was sit there with her eyes focused on the vast field of the dead. Happy she could still move her eyes, her attention zoned to the words coming to her. There were no echoes, just a clear and distinct voice that engendered a vision of a prophet in the wilderness. She listened on.

> "In this field, misfortune and evil abound,
> The dreams of the weak forever suspended.
> What was once of sense and sane no longer abide,
> And a loot in blood leaves the vampire's thirst avast.
> What is so near for many, Satan sees afar.
> How holy they deemed themselves in blood
> When they cast their ills on others and
> Feast on flesh that fills their mouths with blood.
> Look not farther, for there lay the products of cursed wombs
> Conceived the day the Sabbath was defiled.
> And in the lies of them that they behold in honor,
> Their mothers the unholy donors of souls to Satan."

She could not help but listen to the words as they came across to her repeatedly amidst the cries of children that irritated her ears. Unfortunately, she could not even move her hands no matter how much she wished she could shield her ears from the cries. As she sat helplessly, she repeatedly heard, amidst the cries that only got louder and louder,

> "For the deeds done and lies told,
> For your lies and your deeds,
> For our blood that you shed,
> For the ills you have done on this land,
> For your defilement of our land and people,
> For your lies and your evil deeds,
> Your agony will be prolonged and your curse eterne."

This went on and on that she neared madness. She wished so much that she could shut both her ears with her hands and rest her head on her knees; however, it was as if she was forced to bear the burden of listening to the tormenting sound. Tears ran down her cheeks before she drifted out of consciousness.

CPSIA information can be obtained
at www.ICGtesting.com
Printed in the USA
LVHW041159171120
671900LV00006B/514